Forbidden love . . .

"What kind of friend would hit on my sister?" Brian demanded. "How could Aaron do that?"

Chris looked at me. *Should I leave?* his eyes asked. I shook my head. It felt as if we were connected somehow, as if we each knew what the other was thinking.

"I swear I'm gonna kill Aaron," Brian went on.

"Nah," Chris said, giving my brother a friendly smack on the back. "Aaron was just trying to impress Dana. Let it go."

"I won't let it go," Brian snapped. "A real friend wouldn't try to hit on my sister. A *real* friend doesn't do stuff like that. Right, Chris?"

I watched Chris's face get pale. "I guess not," he murmured.

Brian turned to me. "You stay away from Aaron," he ordered. "In fact, stay away from *all* of my friends. Consider them off-limits."

Chris shot me a nervous look. *What about us?* his eyes asked.

"Give me a break, Brian!" I laughed. "You're friends with practically the entire senior class!"

"I'm serious, Dana," Brian said. "Just stay away from my frie~~nds~~. And I'll make sure they stay away from you."

Don't miss any of the books in *Love Stories*
—the romantic series from Bantam Books!

Our
Secret
Love

Miranda Harry

BANTAM BOOKS
NEW YORK · TORONTO · LONDON · SYDNEY · AUCKLAND

RL 6, age 12 and up

OUR SECRET LOVE
A Bantam Book / March 1998

Produced by Daniel Weiss Associates, Inc.
33 West 17th Street
New York, NY 10011.
Cover photography by Michael Segal.

ISBN: 0-553-48592-X

Published simultaneously in the United States and Canada

Bantam Books are published by Bantam Books, a division of Bantam
Doubleday Dell Publishing Group, Inc. Its trademark, consisting of the
words "Bantam Books" and the portrayal of a rooster, is Registered in
U.S. Patent and Trademark Office and in other countries. Marca
Registrada. Bantam Books, 1540 Broadway, New York, New York 10036.

PRINTED IN THE UNITED STATES OF AMERICA

OPM   0 9 8 7 6 5 4 3 2 1

One

M Y BEST FRIEND, Kim, says one of the good things about having an older brother is that he can help you meet a lot of guys. I guess that might be true for some people, but I'd spent so much time with my brother Brian's friends that they were like family. They didn't even bother to be polite around me. I mean, they were pigs! They drank milk straight from the container, and they held belching contests and made me be the judge. So obviously, Brian's friends just felt like extra brothers to me. I'd never really thought of them as *dateable*.

"You think *they're* boyfriend material?" I asked Kim. It was Friday, and we were sitting near the football field after school. It was one of those super-hot Atlanta fall afternoons when you can't imagine ever wearing a sweater again.

"Why not?" she asked, nodding toward my

brother and his friends Chris and Aaron, who were walking across the field to us. "They're only two years older than we are, which is perfect. Not to mention that some of them are extremely cute." Kim cocked her head to the side, a thoughtful expression on her face. "Yeah, I could easily see myself going out with one of them."

"Okay, so *you* could see yourself with them. But come on—what would a senior guy want with a sophomore girl?" I demanded, gathering my thick brown hair into a ponytail. "Especially a sophomore girl like you or me."

Kim shrugged, not bothered by my reminder of the fact that we weren't exactly members of the coolest crowd on campus. "Lots of things. Don't sell yourself short, girlfriend." She smiled. "Remember," she added, "girls mature much faster than boys. Technically, we're the same mental age as Brian and his friends. Maybe older!"

"Maybe," I said. Back when I was little and thought all boys were jerks, my grandmother used to say, "Be patient and they'll catch up to you," promising me that one day boys would occupy nearly all my thoughts. By the time I turned thirteen, Grandma's promise rang true. But my appreciation for guys had gotten me nowhere—I'd never had a serious boyfriend. By the way, neither had Kim—even though she calls *me* a late bloomer, since she became obsessed with guys when she was ten.

I glanced across the field. My brother and his friends were clowning around as they walked. I waved to Brian, and he and Chris waved back. Aaron was too busy trying to simultaneously walk and read the sports section to notice us. He was Brian and Chris's new friend. I got the impression that my brother didn't really like him all that much.

"See, Aaron's kind of sketchy," Kim whispered, even though the three guys were still very far away. "But your brother has gorgeous eyes, and Chris, well, what a body! And check out his hair, his eyebrows . . ."

"His eyebrows!" I laughed. Kim has a tendency to get carried away.

"Good eyebrows are a sign of good character," Kim argued. "You know, Dana, sometimes everything you're looking for is right in front of you."

I rolled my eyes. "You sound like a fortune cookie."

"Whatever." Kim continued to gaze at my brother and his friends. "Fortune cookie or not, take another look at Mr. Chris Geller. I'm just stating the obvious."

Chris was striding toward us, his black hair blowing off his face. Okay, so she *did* have a point. Chris had the best body of any guy I knew, built but not bulky like a weight lifter's. Plus, he had smooth olive skin and beautiful brown eyes. That's why the girls fell all over him.

There's actually a list of Chris's ex-girlfriends scrawled on the wall of the girls' bathroom near the cafeteria. The latest ex posts her name and something about why she now hates Chris Geller. Last time I checked, it was ten names long. Chris has always been really sweet to me, though—and he's a *great* friend to Brian. So looking at that list always made me feel funny—I couldn't imagine Chris being a jerk to anyone.

But then, I also could never understand why all those girls were attracted to Chris in the first place. Didn't they know that he was a slob? Sometimes he wore the same sweaty T-shirt for an entire weekend! He and Brian would lie around our den watching cartoons for hours every Saturday. Why would anyone want to date either of them?

"Chris *is* good-looking," I admitted. "But I just don't think of him that way—he's Brian's best friend. I know him too well to care what he looks like."

Kim stared at me as if I were the stupidest person alive. "You are so blind," she said, shaking her head. "Chris is *fine*. How could you not look at him that way?"

I laughed. "Kim, Chris is like a brother," I explained. "I mean, I've known him since I was ten. He and Brian have been best friends since they were twelve years old. Why are *you* so interested in him anyway?" I searched her face. "Do you like him or something?"

Kim arched her eyebrows in surprise. "Me? No, he's not my type. I'm more interested in . . ." Her voice trailed off as she squinted into the distance. "Never mind. Anyway, I can't date a guy who's more than a foot taller than me. I'd get a stiff neck looking up at him and then my dance teacher would yell at me for being too rigid. But he'd be perfect for *you*."

"Oh yeah?" I said in an amused tone. As usual, Kim was not letting this one go. "Why's that?"

"Well, you're both on the track team, you like the same music, and you've already been hanging out together for years."

"Since when did you become a dating service?" I asked suspiciously.

Kim turned her back to the guys, removed a mirror from her bag, and checked her makeup.

"Besides," she added, ignoring my last comment, "I think he has a thing for you."

"No way," I said, watching Chris approach. "Do you think?"

"Yeah, I do," she said quietly. She grinned at me. "Do I look okay?" she asked.

"Beautiful," I told her truthfully. "You always look great."

I meant it. I've never seen Kim look anything but beautiful. She has the most amazing long hair. It's curly and soft and the color of apricots—like something you'd see in a shampoo ad. I, on the other hand, have regular straight brown hair that automatically stops growing when it hits my shoulders. Kim's also got naturally thick eyelashes that frame her light blue eyes. She's thin and graceful—but muscular, because she takes dance class four mornings a week before school. I prefer running and basketball to rhythm and ballet. I have a more athletic build.

5

Kim's always telling me how gorgeous *I* am, but she's my best friend, so of course she thinks that. I do know that I look healthy and strong, and that makes me happy.

The best thing about Kim is that she's the most honest person you'll ever meet. She would never lie to a friend or cheat on a test or even consider keeping a lost wallet she found on the street. You'd think guys would be asking her out all the time, but so far nobody has. My theory is that they're intimidated by how beautiful she is, or that they figure anyone so beautiful has to have an attitude.

"Ahh!" With a happy yowl, Chris slid onto the grass next to me as if he were sliding into home plate. Kim tucked her mirror in her bag and shot me a knowing smile.

I stuck my tongue out at Kim, but smiled down at Chris. Then I cupped my hands over my mouth to make my voice sound as if it were coming out of a megaphone. "And it's Geller, winning the game for the Atlanta Braves."

"I *am* the most valuable player of all time," Chris said, his brown eyes glittering as he smiled back at me. *Okay,* I repeated silently to myself. *Kim's right. He is cute, especially when his cheeks are all flushed and—*

"Hey, you guys," my brother greeted Kim and me, breaking into my thoughts. Aaron stood right behind him.

"Hi, Bri." I smiled, trying to cover up the embarrassment I felt over my silly thoughts.

6

Aaron plopped down and spread out his newspaper. Brian threw his book bag next to Kim and sprawled out facedown in the grass.

"Tired?" she asked him.

"Wrecked," he moaned. "Fridays ruin me. I need a three-hour nap to make up for waking up at the crack of dawn five days in a row."

"Me too," Kim said, checking her watch and gathering her stuff. "But I have to go to work."

"You work on Fridays?" Chris asked.

"Yeah. From four till ten."

When she's not rehearsing for a dance recital, Kim works at a clothing store in the mall. I don't know how she does everything and still keeps an A average. I work pretty hard, but I could never be as high an achiever as Kim.

"That must be rough," Brian commented. "Working on nap day."

"The money's good," Kim said. "And with cash, I get to do fun things with you guys again. Like, soon, I hope."

"Anytime," Brian replied.

"Dana, are you coming with me to the mall, or are you hanging here?" Kim asked as she climbed to her feet.

I squinted up at her. "Can I pick up some clothes with your discount?"

"Yeah, sure," Kim said, brushing the grass off her plaid skirt.

I stood up and stretched. "Cool. I'm coming, then."

"But I just got here," Chris complained dramatically, clutching my leg from below. "Don't leave me, please!"

"You are such a doofus," I said, untangling myself from his grasp. "We have to catch the next bus or Kim will be late."

"Oh." Chris nodded. "How long are you going to be at the mall?"

I shrugged. "I don't know. A few hours, I guess. Maybe until seven."

Kim put her hands on her hips. "Why do you ask, Chris?"

I glared at Kim. I knew she was trying to lead Chris to admit his "feelings" for me, even though they were nonexistent, a figment of Kim's overactive imagination. I leaned my body into hers as a signal to shut up.

"No reason," Chris said. "Just wondering. Maybe I'll catch you guys later."

Brian sat up from his collapsed position and frowned at me. "How are you getting home from the mall?"

"I don't know—the bus, I guess. Or maybe I'll run into someone I know who'll give me a ride." I grabbed my backpack from the ground.

Brian tends to be very overprotective. This is partly because he's a terrific older brother—the kind who never gets impatient or makes me feel excluded—and partly because I was really sick as a little kid. I had leukemia, so now he takes extra-good care of me. Sometimes I'm grateful, like when I get to

8

hang out with him and his friends. Other times I'm annoyed, like when he acts like a worried parent.

"Well," Brian said, "maybe I should come get you—"

"I'll give you a ride, Dana," Aaron interrupted, looking up for the first time.

I glanced at him in surprise, squaring my backpack on my shoulders. He had an angular, kind of sneering face that some girls would find attractive, but he wasn't my type. He must have been sweltering in his leather jacket, boots, and oversize jeans, but there's no way he'd ever let on. I knew that he was the type of guy who tried to play it cool at all times.

"I'll be at the mall later anyway," he explained, running a hand through his hair. "I can swing by and pick you up at seven-thirty by the main entrance."

Chris's eyes opened wide. And Brian definitely looked worried. Apparently, he didn't trust Aaron all that much. But neither of them said anything.

"Okay. Thanks," I told Aaron. I decided to ignore Brian's and Chris's bizarre reaction. After all, I needed a ride. "See you guys later," I called over my shoulder as Kim led me away.

"See ya," my brother called back. "Be careful."

When Kim and I were safely out of earshot she turned to me. "I saw that."

"What?"

"Chris was bummed when Aaron said he'd drive you home tonight," she said.

"Yeah, well, Brian seemed weird too. What's your point?"

9

"My point is that Chris is into you, Dana," she said in an exasperated tone. "The way he always sits next to you, talks to you, wants to know what you're up to—"

"I don't think so," I interrupted as we reached the concrete walkway that led to the bus stop. "He hasn't been treating me any differently than he always does. He's *always* been nice to me, Kim."

Kim shook her head. "All I can say is he seemed really interested in your plans. And when you were talking to Aaron, he didn't take his eyes off you for one second."

"You were watching?"

"Of course." She put her arm around me. "Somebody has to pay attention to these things, since you don't."

Kim plopped down onto the wooden bench at the bus stop. I sat next to her, thinking about what she said.

Chris really hadn't taken his eyes off me? A shiver of excitement ran down my spine. Maybe Kim *was* on to something. Maybe I had been too preoccupied to notice.

"Really?" I asked. "You really think there's something there?"

"Definite sexual energy," she said emphatically. "No doubt about it."

I smiled to myself as the bus pulled to a stop in front of us. For a brief moment, I saw Chris Geller in a whole new light.

★ ★ ★

But that moment didn't last long. After all, everyone knew Chris was a big flirt. Brian said Chris had already gone out with nearly every girl in his chemistry class, and it was only October. So, by the time the bus dropped Kim and me off in front of the mall, I had decided that Chris had "definite sexual energy" with lots of girls. Yes, I realized as we looked through the racks at Anthropology, the store she worked at, Kim was making a big deal out of nothing.

Kim gets a forty-percent discount on everything Anthropology sells. That, on top of the Columbus Day sale, meant I could get some new clothes supercheap. I took three pairs of jeans into the dressing room, and Kim tossed a shiny brown miniskirt over the door.

"Try this," she urged. "Show off your fabulous legs."

"You know I'm not really into skirts," I called. I like more comfortable clothes—jeans and flannel shirts. I hardly ever dress up.

"I think it's time you got into skirts," Kim announced, opening my dressing room door a crack and handing me a yellow-and-green patterned blouse.

"Well . . ."

"Trust me. It's my job to know these things." She closed the door and waited in front of it. The door stopped about six inches short of the floor, and I could see Kim tapping her foot in anticipation.

I slipped on the miniskirt and funky blouse, cautiously emerged from the dressing room, and presented myself to Kim. "Well?" I asked.

11

"Fantastic," she declared, shoving me toward a full-length mirror. "Look at you!"

"You think?" I studied my reflection. Lately I'd been running three miles every morning before school, so I *was* in pretty good shape.

"Shows off your best features. Your legs and your boobs."

I felt the blood rush to my cheeks. *"Kim."* I whipped around and glared at her, covering my chest with my arms.

Kim shrugged. "All I'm saying is you got it, so you might as well flaunt it. And I bet Chris will love you in that outfit."

I sighed. "Will you cut it out with this Chris-has-a-crush-on-me thing? Don't you have other customers to attend to or anything?"

Kim looked startled. "All right, all right, relax. But believe me—you look killer in that outfit." She picked up a pair of scissors. "Do you want to take it?"

I nodded. "I guess so. If you really think it looks good."

"I do. Keep it on." She cut off the price tags with the scissors. "I'll ring you up and put your other clothes in a shopping bag."

"Thanks." I handed her two twenty-dollar bills.

"No problem." She headed toward the register.

When she was out of sight, I sneaked another look at myself in the mirror, shifting my weight from one leg to the other, scrutinizing my profile and my posture.

There had been a time when I refused to look at my reflection because I couldn't believe what I saw— a swollen, hairless, pasty-faced, unrecognizable sick person. But that was eight years ago, and that was because I had leukemia. Now, I'm completely cured. Medicine is truly amazing—the way it saved me is what has inspired me to want to be a doctor. I took a deep breath, once again thankful for my good health.

Then I stood up straighter and smiled at my reflection. I had to admit, I felt beautiful.

Kim returned with a sales slip, a pair of chunky sandals, and a plastic shopping bag in which she'd stuffed the clothes I wore to school. "I hope Chris is hanging out with Brian at your house tonight so that he can see how terrific you look."

Goose bumps ran up my arm when she said that. An image popped into my mind: I would walk into my house and find Chris sitting in the den as usual, watching a video on our big-screen TV. Brian would be conveniently out of the way, still taking his Friday afternoon nap upstairs. I'd stand in the doorway and Chris's attention would immediately shift from the TV to me. He'd look at me and smile. Then he'd come toward me and tell me he'd never noticed how beautiful I was and shyly ask if it would be all right to kiss me. And then . . .

Then he would open his mouth and burp in my face, I reminded myself. What was I doing, thinking about Chris this way?

"Dana, hello—are you with us?" Kim dangled the sandals in front of me. I must have looked embarrassed, because she said, "Having a little private moment with Chris?"

"What are you, a mind reader?" I quickly grabbed the sandals and slipped them on, handing her the shoes I'd been wearing.

"No—I don't have to be. It's written all over your face."

I shook my head defiantly. "I'm just spacey, that's all. You know, it's Friday."

"Mmm," she said, disbelief evident in her tone. "Okay, then. You go home and rest up. I'll talk to you tomorrow."

"Thanks for the discount," I told her. I turned to leave.

"Sweet dreams," she called after me.

I laughed as I walked into the mall. She was *not* going to let it go!

But as I clicked across the shiny mall floor in my new sandals, I realized that the truth was the truth—there was no denying how I felt. I didn't totally understand it, but I had to admit they were there, these strange feelings for Chris Geller. Had they been there for a while and I just hadn't noticed? Had Kim's suggestions made me realize how I felt?

I sighed, shaking my head. Who knew? I looked down at my watch: 7:20. I did know one thing: A ride home with Aaron would be much faster than the bus, and I was very eager to get home. Chris might be there. Suddenly, I couldn't wait to see him.

Two

"I SHOULD HAVE just taken the bus," I muttered, rubbing my hands up my arms to keep warm. I had been standing outside the main entrance of the mall for twenty minutes. Aaron was nowhere in sight. A cold breeze had replaced the hot afternoon air and I didn't have a jacket. I checked my watch for the tenth time. Where was he?

At eight o'clock I finally decided to call home for a ride. I had just pulled open the big glass door to the mall when I spotted Aaron's black convertible. He came to a loud, screeching stop directly in front of me, polluting the clean night air with exhaust fumes.

Aaron, adorned in a black T-shirt and black jeans, leaned across the front seat and opened the passenger door. He gave a low whistle and nodded at my new clothes. "Nice."

I felt myself blush. I hoped Aaron didn't think I

was all dressed up for *him*. "Thanks," I said, quickly sliding into the car.

"Cold?" Aaron asked.

"A little."

"Here." He threw his black leather jacket on my lap.

"Uh, thanks. What took you so long?" I asked.

"Gas."

"Gas?" I repeated.

"There was a line," he said, screeching out of the parking lot.

A half-hour line? I wondered, sitting back in my seat.

The ride got off to a pretty bad start. And it didn't get any better. Aaron sped around corners as I shivered in the front seat beneath his leather jacket. After several minutes of silence, Aaron asked, "Are you hungry?"

My stomach had started to feel rather empty. I hadn't eaten since the bagel I had for lunch. "Sort of," I said, thinking we could catch a drive-through window on our way to my house.

"We could stop off at Houston's," he suggested. "It's on the way."

I was surprised. I mean, Houston's is a great restaurant. It's casual but not a total dump, and the food is always good—burgers and nachos and huge salads and stuff. There's always a lot of seniors from my high school there. It's one of my brother's favorite spots—I often went there with him and Chris.

"Well, okay," I agreed. Maybe I'd even run into Brian and Chris there and catch a ride home with them. "That shouldn't take long."

16

"In a hurry?" Aaron sounded annoyed.

"Uh, no. I've just got a bunch of things to do at home," I said.

Aaron didn't respond. He got on the freeway and took the car up to eighty miles an hour. The top was still down—I had to hold my hair to my head to keep it from getting into a completely tangled mess.

Thankfully, traffic forced him to ride the brake for a while.

He said something I couldn't hear.

"What?" I yelled. I reached over to turn down the loud rap music blaring from his radio.

"Stupid traffic," Aaron said. "I was cruising." He turned the music back up—louder than before.

As I tried to tune out the sounds, I began to wonder what I was doing in Aaron's car in the first place. I'd never really hung out with Aaron before. Now I was starting to see why Brian wasn't crazy about him. Brian said he could be a lot of fun, but he could also be selfish. Well, I was seeing the selfish side—and the fun side was nowhere in sight.

I glanced over at Aaron. His hair flew in the wind and his hands thumped on the steering wheel to the beat of the music. He swerved in and out of traffic, cutting off a Honda driven by a guy with white hair and a beard.

"Be careful!" I cried.

Aaron just laughed.

Ugh, I thought. *But think positive—maybe dinner won't take long.*

*   *   *

So much for the power of optimism. There was a half-hour wait at Houston's.

"Look, I really should get home," I told Aaron. "Why don't we just skip—"

"Nah, the wait is never as long as they say it is," Aaron interrupted.

"Here's your beeper," the hostess said. She held out a small blue pager. "It will vibrate when your table is ready."

I reached for the beeper, but Aaron snatched it out of her hand. "Hey, can you put us in front of those other people on the list?" he asked her.

"No," the hostess said with a frown. "They were here first. Why don't you guys go wait in the bar?"

I was about to tell her we were too young to sit at the bar, but Aaron grabbed my hand, pushed a few strangers out of our way, and settled us on two empty bar stools.

What am I supposed to do? I wondered. Aaron was being sort of rude. But I wasn't scared or anything. I mean, Brian was friends with this guy. Plus, I didn't want to make a scene. So I decided to ride things out for a while. At least I'd get to eat.

Aaron ordered himself a beer. *This night is getting pretty bad,* I thought.

"Can I see your ID?" asked the bartender. He was wearing a "Hello, I'm Dave, Welcome to Houston's" button. Aaron displayed an obviously fake license without hesitation. The bartender studied the ID for a moment. Then he nodded and

18

popped open a bottle of Budweiser, handing it to Aaron.

"Thanks, *Dave*," Aaron sneered.

"And for you, miss?" Dave asked me.

"Just an orange juice, thanks."

"You have a fake ID?" I said when the bartender had moved on to other customers.

"Yup. Looks real, huh?" Aaron said, proudly showing me a bogus driver's license with his picture on it: Jerry Schuler, California, born September 3, 1976.

"Definitely looks real," I answered insincerely. Obviously, Aaron didn't realize the fake ID made him look like a jerk. What did Brian and Chris see in this guy? He was totally unimpressive. Aaron began drinking his beer in huge gulps. I scanned the room, hoping to see someone I knew who I could bum a ride with.

"So," Aaron said between swallows, "tell me a little something about Dana Lipton."

What a line! I had to hold myself back from laughing. It was almost as if he were hitting on me.

"What do you want to know?" I asked.

Aaron leered at me. "Well, I know you're Brian Lipton's sister, and he's a cool guy, so it probably runs in the family."

"Uh, yeah," I said cautiously.

"And I know you're really athletic, and Brian's definitely not."

"Right. That doesn't run in the family," I said.

Aaron took another swig and wiped his mouth

with the back of his hand. "Actually, I just met your brother's friend Chris this semester, so we're not really that close. But we hang out sometimes."

"Oh." What was he trying to say?

"I bet kids used to make fun of your last name. You know, like the tea? Cup-A-Soup?"

"Yeah," I said unenthusiastically. The alcohol had made Aaron talkative. But I couldn't really figure out what he was getting at.

"So, what else?"

I felt uncomfortable—I mean, was he expecting me to tell him my IQ? My dreams and goals? My best and worst qualities? I wanted to get out of there. But so far I hadn't spotted anyone I knew. Aaron was still my only hope for a ride home.

"Well," I said, gazing at the crowded dining room. "I really love Houston's." That was honest.

"Yeah," he agreed.

"And I hate not being able to drive."

He looked me up and down. "It can't be that bad when you can get a ride with me," he said.

I laughed—I couldn't help it. He wasn't serious, was he? Then I saw the look on his face and I knew he *was* serious. He was hitting on me! And this guy was a friend of Brian's?

Thankfully, our beeper vibrated, and I jumped off the bar stool.

"Hey, Dave," Aaron called to the bartender. "Send another beer to my table."

Oh, wonderful, I thought. Now I was getting worried. How was he supposed to drive home if he was drinking? Maybe I could make him stop after two. Maybe I should call my parents. . . .

We followed the hostess through the massive crowd to a small table in the corner. Aaron saw some friends of his along the way, and he stopped to say hi and steal french fries off their plates.

"This is Dana," he said, presenting me to a group of seniors I recognized but didn't know. "She's Brian Lipton's little sister."

A skinny blond guy stood up. "Hey there, Brian Lipton's little sister."

I smiled, though it wasn't easy. I felt like an idiot. The tall blond guy nudged Aaron in the ribs and Aaron grinned.

"Doesn't she talk?" he asked Aaron, as if I weren't right there in front of them.

"Only to people she likes."

"Hello," I said loudly.

"Guess she likes *me*," the guy said. His girl-friend grabbed his arm and pulled him back down to his seat.

I wanted to disappear. Aaron was acting so strange. Besides, this was clearly an all-seniors crowd, and without my brother or Chris, I was totally out of place.

The hostess was growing impatient. She pointed at our table and walked away, so I pulled Aaron gently by his jacket. "Later," he said to his friends.

He threw himself into his seat and stared at me.

"You know," he said, leaning across the table, his face close to mine, "if I didn't know you were

Brian's little sister . . ." He shook his head. "Well anyway."

I took a sip of my water. I didn't want to know where *that* thought led. "Well, thanks for giving me a ride," I replied, trying to stress the fact that this whole night meant nothing more to me than transportation and a little food. Which I intended to pay for myself.

"The only other sophomore I ever went out with was Joanna Winterson," he said thoughtfully. "She was pretty cool."

The only other sophomore he ever *went out with?* I couldn't believe this! He thought this was a date! I needed to end it as quickly as possible.

The waiter brought Aaron's second beer and the menus. I scanned mine to find the meals that would require the least amount of time to prepare. I narrowed it down to three options: onion soup, which is cooked in huge pots and sits on the stove all night; nachos, which they probably just threw into the microwave; and salads. How long could it take to throw together a salad?

"I'll have the oriental chicken salad," I said when our waiter returned.

"Bacon cheeseburger," Aaron ordered. "Well done. And potato skins."

The waiter scribbled down our order and proceeded to another table. *Terrific,* I thought. The burger would take at least ten minutes, the skins even longer. Plus, the place was packed. I was going to be stuck there for a while.

"So, I figured we could take a drive after dinner," Aaron told me.

"Well, I'd really love a drive home," I replied.

Aaron laughed. Did he think I was kidding? "I know this place outside the city," he said, raising his eyebrows. "You know, a place that's not so crowded."

"I don't think so." I shook my head.

He looked amused, as if he didn't believe me. "Why not?"

I took a deep breath. "Well, for one thing, Aaron," I began, "this was not supposed to be a date." I checked my watch. "Second, my curfew's in about half an hour, so I can't."

"That stinks about your curfew," Aaron said. Clearly he had chosen to ignore my first comment. "Half an hour?"

"Yup."

"You sure?"

"I'm positive," I said.

"I bet you can stretch it—just a little? I'll make it worth your while," he murmured.

Gross! I thought. *He's getting totally out of control!*

"No. I can't be late," I insisted.

"Great," he said, sounding as annoyed as he had when we'd gotten stuck in traffic. He peeled the label off his beer bottle. Then he slumped back in his chair. "What's the use," he muttered. "Chris probably has first dibs on you anyway." He tilted his head back and downed most of his beer.

"What?" My annoyance suddenly turned into curiosity. "What are you talking about?" Did

23

Aaron pick up on the same vibe Kim did? Nah, I knew better now than to believe anything Aaron said.

"Nothing. I'm talking about absolutely nothing," he said, a strange half smile on his face. Then his eyes focused on something behind me. "Speak of the devil, there's Chris. Down at the other end, see?"

I turned around and saw Chris sitting at a table with Joanna Winterson. My heart leaped in my chest. I was thrilled to see him, until I realized I should be depressed. After all, he was with another girl. I watched as Joanna affectionately picked food off his plate. I'd seen Chris with other girls dozens of times before now, but somehow tonight was different. This time, I noticed things.

For example, I noticed that he had changed into a clean white T-shirt, which made his olive skin look even darker. His hair was perfectly messy, the kind of look it takes time and mousse to achieve. And he was sitting closer to Joanna Winterson than he needed to.

If Kim were here, she'd have caught me staring, but Aaron was too intrigued by the bacon cheeseburger the waiter had set in front of him to notice me glancing at Chris every other second. Now I wished we had ordered appetizers so that I wouldn't have to leave so soon.

"Chris is with your ex," I said, trying to get information and sound uninterested at the same time.

"Joanna is *everybody's* ex," Aaron scowled, squeezing a fist-size dollop of ketchup onto his bun. He chowed down, keeping his eyes on his plate and avoiding eye contact with me.

I glanced over at Chris again—and found him staring back at me, a frown on his face.

Then he stood up and walked toward our table, leaving Joanna Winterson alone to stir her ginger ale with her finger and dart her eyes all over the room.

"Hey, buddy," Chris said, patting Aaron a little too firmly on the back. Aaron nearly choked on his burger. "How's it going?"

"It *was* going good, Chris." Aaron did not look thrilled to see him.

"How are you doing, Dana?" Chris asked, turning to me.

"Okay," I replied. I tried to tell Chris with my eyes that things *weren't* okay, that Aaron was a jerk, and that I wanted out.

Chris didn't need any hints. "How's the beer, Aaron?"

"Fine." Aaron eyed Chris suspiciously.

"How many have you had?"

"You keeping score or something?" Aaron asked defensively.

"Nope. Doesn't matter to me what you do, especially since you're not driving Dana home."

I smiled. *Thank you, Chris. Thank you.*

"Give me a break. I had two beers," Aaron protested. "I can drive her home."

"Don't sweat it, man," Chris said. "I'm headed there anyway to see Brian. What time do you have to be home, Dana?"

I looked up at Chris. "Well, now-ish. Really, Aaron, thanks for the offer, but I should go with Chris." Even if Aaron hadn't been drinking, I wouldn't have missed out on a ride home with Chris.

"Just sit tight here for a second," Chris said, his hands on Aaron's shoulders. "I'll be right back."

"Back off, man," Aaron said, shrugging to get Chris away from him.

"No problem. I'm gone." Chris walked back to his table.

Aaron stared at his burger for a few moments. "I guess Chris will take you home," he muttered.

"Okay," I said neutrally. I really didn't want to humiliate Aaron and I certainly didn't want to make him angrier.

"He's going there anyway," Aaron explained, as if I hadn't been there for the whole conversation. "He's going to see Brian."

"Makes sense," I said, watching Chris return to his table.

Chris leaned over Joanna Winterson, probably explaining the situation to her. Joanna nodded, glared at me, then turned back to Chris. She was so girlish and delicate, with her nail polish and makeup and china-doll face, my total opposite. If Joanna was Chris's type, then Kim was definitely wrong to think he'd ever be into me.

"How did you know I needed to be rescued?" I asked Chris as I buckled my seat belt.

Chris smiled knowingly. "It wasn't hard. Aaron's okay, but not when it comes to girls," he explained.

"Well, thanks a lot," I said, trying to get comfortable in my seat.

"Are you kidding? I'm the one who gets to drive home a gorgeous girl. I should be thanking you!"

That's the first thing girls always say about Chris—he's the smoothest talker around. Even I'd noticed how easily he talked to people. Now I wondered if he was being insincere or genuinely charming.

"I don't know," I said seriously, testing him. "You could have been driving Joanna Winterson home."

"I couldn't have driven her home. We came in separate cars. It wasn't a date or anything," he said emphatically.

I sighed with relief. I uncrossed my legs and opened his glove compartment. It gave me something to do with my hands. For the first time in all the years I'd known Chris, I was feeling nervous around him.

"Really?" I said, trying to sound nonchalant. I poked through a Honda Civic car manual, a tube of unscented Chap Stick, and a half-eaten bag of strawberry licorice. I don't know what special signs I expected to find in there, but since I'd never been inside Chris's house or seen much of his personal stuff, I thought maybe these little details might reveal something about him. Maybe if I found some

27

girl's phone number or directions to her house, I'd have some clue as to what he did when he wasn't with my brother.

"Joanna and I have gone out a few times, but it's really casual," Chris went on, as if he needed to explain her to me. "She and Aaron still have this unresolved thing going on, which is probably why she agreed to drive him home when I explained he'd been drinking." I glanced up at him, trying to read his expression. "What are you looking for anyway?" he asked, grinning.

"Food. I barely touched my dinner," I lied, biting into a licorice stick and offering him the other half. "It was pretty cool of Joanna to let you ditch her like that."

"I didn't ditch her," he corrected, taking the licorice stick from me. "We were there with a bunch of people in the first place, and we were finished eating. Everyone else left to go to some keg party in Buckhead. I hadn't made any plans with her to do anything else." He rolled down the window a little bit. "Besides, we're just friends," Chris repeated.

Was he telling the truth? I decided to believe him. After all, why would he lie to me? I leaned back in my seat, suddenly feeling silly for being nervous. *Relax,* I told myself. *This is Chris. I have nothing to hide . . . or do I?*

He reached over, took a Scorching Stones CD out of the glove compartment, and popped it in the portable CD player. "Joanna's a nice girl and everything," he said, "but she's nothing special."

I sat up straight again. This caught my attention. "What do you mean she's nothing special?" I asked. I couldn't help wondering just what Chris considered "special."

"You know, she doesn't have any special interests. Like sports or music or anything. She's just sort of . . . *there*." Chris shrugged. "Not a lot of depth."

"Huh." I nodded. It had never occurred to me that Chris cared if his girlfriends had depth.

The music came on and Chris glanced at me. "You're a Scorching Stones fan, right?" he asked.

"Definitely," I said, turning up the volume. "They're my favorite new group. I love 'Tidal Wave' and 'When I'm with You.' "

Chris shook his head. "I always told your brother that you had good taste."

I smiled at the compliment. "I'm dying to see them in concert—everyone says they're awesome live," I said. "I heard they're coming back to Atlanta soon, but that might just be a rumor."

Everyone had been talking about Scorching Stones lately. They're a local band—I don't think anyone outside of Georgia has heard of them. But here, the college radio stations play their CD constantly, and the band's been known to show up unannounced and do late-night gigs at local clubs. The drummer graduated from our high school, so everyone seems to feel a personal connection to the group.

"I heard that too," Chris said, driving toward

the highway. "I'm going to call a friend of mine who works at a music store and see if he can score us some tickets."

Us? Him and his friend, or him and me? There was an awkward pause while I evaluated the possibilities. I would love to go to a concert with Chris more than anything. But then, so would every other girl I know.

"What are you thinking?" he asked.

I glanced over at him. "That a lot of girls would kill to be where I am, in a car with Chris Geller," I said, unashamed. After all, he *was* like a brother to me. No reason not to tell him exactly what was in my head.

He laughed. "You sure are blunt."

"I'm just telling the truth as I know it," I replied.

A thoughtful expression spread across his face as he stared at the road. I noticed for the first time that Chris had a nice profile, strong and definite.

"You only live once, right? So speak your mind. Is that it?"

"Exactly," I said.

That sounds like a cheesy cliché: "You only live once." But it's a truth I learned firsthand. Fighting leukemia changed the way I thought about my life. It made me more courageous, I guess, than a lot of people my age. I want to be brave, say what I believe, go for things I really want. I'm not always successful, and sometimes I'm really scared, but I always try. I know another cliché that turned out to be true: Anything that doesn't kill you makes you stronger. For me, six months in a hospital cancer ward helped make me a stronger person. Everything about that time and place was terrifying. Even the regular blood tests I had to take after I got out of the hospital scared me. Then, when the doctors told me I was cured, I made a promise to myself to be as fearless as I could be. That's why I was the only freshman who tried out for the basketball team, and why I'm planning to go rock climbing next summer.

Chris knew I'd had leukemia, but I didn't think he knew any details. I doubted that Brian would have told him much about those days. My brother is usually quiet about things that upset him. I'm sure he just wants to forget about the whole thing. And I don't talk about my illness unless someone asks. Even then, I'm pretty reluctant to go into detail about it. I try to put those bad memories far behind me.

"If you're so bold," Chris said, turning down the stereo, "why didn't you say no to Aaron when he asked you out?"

"He didn't ask me out," I protested. "He just offered me a ride home."

"Uh-huh," Chris said.

"I'm serious! You were there!"

"And you didn't think anything of it?"

"Well, *you've* offered me a ride hundreds of times and I never thought anything about that either."

"It's different," he said.

"How?" I pressed.

"Aaron is sort of an idiot, for one thing. And I'm not."

"Well, thanks for warning me," I said irritably. Now that I thought about it, I was angry at Brian and Chris for keeping their mouths shut.

"I tried to, but you had already said yes."

"So?" Had everyone but me known that Aaron's offer was a date in disguise? "I could have changed my mind."

"Well, I wanted to do something, maybe offer to drive you home myself, but I thought it was too late."

I frowned. "At least you showed up at Houston's."

Chris laughed. "I had a feeling he might take you there." He paused. "I don't want someone, you know, taking advantage of you or anything. That's what I was thinking anyway."

"Well, if you were so worried—not that I can't take care of myself—you should have been more daring and said something right away," I egged him on. "You know, rescued me."

"Be your knight in shining armor?"

"That would be nice."

"I'll have to remember that," he joked. "I'll be more bold next time."

I'd never had a conversation like this with Chris. I mean, we were *flirting*. My entire body pounded with excitement.

"Be bold now," I challenged him. "Tell me exactly what you're thinking, without censoring yourself."

There was silence between us, like the calm before a thunderclap. I held my breath and waited. Chris exhaled loudly as if he too had been unable to breathe for a moment.

"You look fantastic," he blurted out. "There. I said it."

"Thank you," I said. I was flattered. I was also a nervous wreck. What was I doing? Chris was— well, *Chris!* My brother's best friend. *My* friend.

"You look fantastic, and I think you're, well, not just good-looking on the surface but totally, thoroughly beautiful."

I sat there, stunned. I looked at my bare legs and new sandals. No more hiding under sweatpants and flannel shirts around Chris Geller. Totally, thoroughly beautiful? That wasn't something you just *said.* There was something behind those words—I knew it. And I could feel the atmosphere in the car transforming into something significant. My surrogate older brother had just become something *more.*

"Are you serious? That's what you were thinking?" I asked.

"Yes," he admitted. "Dana, there's something about you that seems so . . ." He hesitated, searching for the right word. "Substantial. I know you went through some pretty tough stuff when you were little. I don't know the details, but all I can say is I think you're somehow special because of it. You're not just some immature sophomore who doesn't have a clue. You care about more than makeup and hairstyles. You run deeper." He studied me for a reaction, and I nodded shyly.

"All I know is that lately I've really liked being with you," he went on. "A lot more than usual, and I want to get to know you better. You're much more than my best friend's little sister. Does this make sense?"

It made total sense. Ever since I got sick, I've felt like an outsider witnessing a world that would never understand me. Other people's priorities were making good grades and getting dates and being popular. Mine were being grateful for my family and friends, doing my best, and appreciating each healthy day. I never expected Chris Geller would be the one person—besides my family and Kim—to notice I was different. The one person to admire me for being me.

We stopped at a red light and Chris turned to look at me with an energy so intense I thought it would consume me. I looked back, unashamed of what I was feeling, what he must have known I was feeling. I wanted to sit in that car with Chris all night. All of a sudden, I was falling in love.

Three

"WHAT HAPPENED TO Aaron?" Brian asked as I unlocked the front door, Chris standing beside me. Brian sat on the carpeted stairs just inside, his arms folded across his chest, obviously waiting for me. "And why are you over an hour late?"

"Aaron got tied up, Bri," Chris replied. "What are you doing anyway? It looks like you're waiting for a bus."

I giggled. Brian did look silly just sitting there.

"Tied up?" he asked suspiciously. "What, did he not show up or something?"

"No, he showed up," I said, walking past Brian down the narrow hallway and into the kitchen. Chris followed. To my surprise, my parents were sitting at the kitchen table, pretending to read the newspaper.

"Everything okay?" my dad asked, looking up

35

from the crossword puzzle. "I know you wouldn't miss curfew without a good reason."

"I'm fine," I replied. "Sorry I'm late."

"Hello, Christopher. Don't you look nice, Dana," my mother said, kissing me on the cheek.

"Thanks, Mom." I love my mother. She's always calm and serene, as if she finds everything in life to be beautiful. She never wears makeup, and her dark hair is short and loose around her face. Even though she just turned forty, she looks young enough to be my big sister. My dad, who's only forty-three, looks much more like a dad than Mom looks like a mom. Deep creases in his forehead make him look worried, even when he's not. Brian inherited those worry lines, and I have a few traces of them. People say I look more like my mom, though. I love my dad and all, but I hope they're right.

"Bad date, huh?" Dad commiserated. He's a guidance counselor at a private school, so he tries to be aware of teenagers' troubles. He's one of those cut-to-the-chase dads, unlike some of my friends' fathers who don't know anything about what's really going on in their kids' lives.

"Not really. Not really a date, I mean," I said, noticing the bright yellow teakettle puffing steam on the stove. "Anyone want some peppermint tea?"

My parents and Chris nodded.

"And?" Brian pressed. He sounded really annoyed. "So? Where is he? What happened?" he asked.

I took four tea bags from the glass mason jar (my mom has a counter full of jars for everything—tea, cocoa, pasta, lentils, you name it) and arranged them in four small mugs. "Aaron picked me up late. We went to Houston's on the way home," I said quickly. "We ran into Chris and Joanna Winterson. Aaron drank a beer and Chris thought he shouldn't drive. So Joanna Winterson drove Aaron home and Chris gave me a ride. End of story."

I looked Brian in the eye, warning him to drop the subject. He didn't flinch.

"Chris," my dad said, scratching his sand-colored beard, "we owe you one."

"You bet we do," my mother echoed.

"Nah—it's the least I can do, Mr. and Mrs. Lipton," Chris said, taking a cookie off the plate on the table. "You let me eat dinner here practically every night."

My parents smiled. Neither of them looked too upset.

But Brian was fuming. Even his ears were red. "What's the matter with Aaron? He offers her a ride and then he gets too drunk to drive? He should have taken her right home. Why did he have to stop for food?"

"Guess your friends aren't always so responsible," Dad said in his most guidance counselor tone, as if this incident should teach all of us a lesson.

"Yeah, whatever," Brian agreed, looking at the floor.

My father continued. "Guess you can't rely on

them to make safe choices. You can only rely on *you* to make safe choices."

Last year at my father's school, three students were killed in drunk driving accidents. He worked nights and weekends to help their classmates cope with the tragedies. Ever since then, drinking and driving is a particularly touchy subject for him, one that leaves no room for debate.

My father looked at me for some expression of agreement. "Right, Dana?"

"Yes, Dad."

"Next time, you'll call for a ride," he said matter-of-factly.

"I promise. I was about to anyway when Chris showed up."

"Stupid idiot," Brian mumbled. I had a feeling he was talking about himself, not Aaron. "I knew it. I never should've let you go with him."

"*Let* me go with him?" I repeated. "Did I need your permission?"

The teakettle began to hiss, which gave me the perfect excuse to turn my back, pour the water, and get a hold of myself. There was no way I'd get into a big fight with Brian in front of Chris. Not tonight.

My mother took two mugs of steaming tea and handed one to my dad. "Everybody's safe and sound, no harm done," she said, consoling both Brian and my dad at the same time. She gestured for my father to follow her upstairs and leave us alone in the kitchen. It's my favorite room in the house, with its cheerful yellow walls and friendly round wooden table. Brian loves it too. But tonight, nothing was going to brighten his mood.

When we heard my parents close their bedroom door, Brian erupted. "I can't believe you, Dana."

"What?" I cried.

"It wasn't her fault," Chris said. "Aaron is a show-off, especially when he's around girls. You know what he's like. Dana didn't do anything wrong."

"He was going to drink and drive!" Brian paced around the kitchen, his sneakers squeaking rhythmically on the tile floor. "I don't need to almost lose my sister again, thank you very much."

Chris and I knew that Brian was overreacting. He was really thinking about my leukemia—that word nobody ever speaks out loud, as if saying it will cause the disease to come back. Chris looked at me. *Should I leave?* his eyes asked. I shook my head. It felt as if we were connected somehow, as if we each knew what the other was thinking.

"That's not going to happen, Brian," I promised him. "I'm healthy and I'm careful and I'm smart."

"I swear I'm gonna kill Aaron," Brian muttered.

"Nah," Chris said, giving my brother a friendly smack on the back. "Aaron was just trying to impress Dana. Let it go."

"I won't let it go," Brian snapped. "A real friend wouldn't try to hit on my sister. A *real* friend doesn't do stuff like that, right?"

I watched Chris's face get pale. "I guess not," he murmured.

Brian turned to me. "You stay away from Aaron," he ordered. "In fact, stay away from *all* of my friends. Consider them off-limits."

"Give me a break!" I laughed. "You're friends with practically the entire senior class!"

"I'm serious, Dana," he said. "Just stay away from them and I'll make sure they stay away from you."

Chris and I glanced at each other and then away again.

I was overwhelmed with the urge to scream at Brian. How dare he make rules and regulations about my social life? Tonight of all nights. And in front of Chris!

"Oh, okay, Brian," I said, my words dripping with hostility. I busied myself pouring milk in my tea. "So now I'm totally dependent on you. Thanks for taking such good care of me." I had to leave the room. I knew that if I didn't get out of there immediately, I would make a total bawling fool of myself.

I stormed out of the kitchen and headed up to my room. Halfway up the stairs, I stopped to peer over the banister. Chris was watching me helplessly. Brian had just ruined any chance that Chris would make a move for me, and Chris and I both knew it.

"Thanks for taking control of my life," I called. "I know I was really messing it up."

Brian turned and looked up at me. I was hoping he'd take back what he'd said, but his face was set in that I-know-I'm-doing-what's-best-for-you expression he always wears when he's ordering me around.

Brian thinks that he can be totally unreasonable, as long as he has my best interests at heart. I know he's terrified of losing me. And sometimes I appreciate his overprotectiveness. But I didn't need him to watch out for me anymore the way I did when I was a kid. Why couldn't he understand that?

For a moment, I felt sorry for him. But he was butting into my social life when it was none of his business! I didn't care if his heart was in the right place—I just felt angry.

My parents' light was still on, so I knocked quietly on their door and went in. Right away they could see I was troubled.

"You can tell us," Mom encouraged, closing her magazine on her lap. "What's wrong?"

"This whole night is what's wrong. Brian blew the whole thing way out of proportion."

My father patted the end of the bed, motioning for me to sit down. "He worries about you," he said.

"Yeah—too much," I complained. "Now the entire senior class is off-limits to me, thanks to Brian."

Mom reached over and took my hand. "You know how emotional he can be, Dana. Just give him time to calm down."

"I guess," I said, counting in my head the number of days left until I could get my driver's license and really be independent of Brian. Three hundred and twelve. "Can't you talk to him or something?" I asked.

"If that becomes necessary," Dad said, "then of course we will. Meanwhile, you have your school life and basketball and track and your friends. You should focus on them, not on Brian."

I nodded and got up to leave. My parents had totally missed the point, which was that my life suddenly seemed empty compared to the life I might have with Chris.

True, I hadn't given them much to go on. But how do you tell your parents you're starting to care about someone you know really well, in a whole new way?

I went to my room and threw myself on the bed, glaring angrily at the walls. My emotions bounced all over the place—one minute I hated Brian, the next minute I was excited about Chris. And I felt frustrated with my parents for not understanding why I was so upset. Most of all, I was angry at myself for being such a coward.

Why hadn't I confronted Brian with the truth of my feelings for Chris? Why hadn't I told my parents? And I prided myself on being bold and courageous? What a joke! My head began to hurt, so I rolled over on my back and concentrated on the star-filled ceiling.

When I was ten, I had pasted about a hundred glow-in-the-dark stars up there, trying my best to accurately re-create the constellations. It was about a year after I went into remission, and even though I was healthy I felt tired all the time. I had to sneak into my bed for a nap every afternoon.

My bed became my safe haven, and the stars soothed me. Back then, looking at them reminded me there was a huge world waiting for me to enjoy. But tonight, the stars made me feel helpless and all alone in the world.

Totally, thoroughly beautiful, Chris had said. People don't say things like that unless they really mean them. At this very moment, he was downstairs in my kitchen. It was like so many nights before, yet tonight was different. Because tonight I hoped he was thinking about me.

How can I feel this way about him? I wondered. *Why haven't I ever felt like this before? And why did Brian have to pick this night to forbid me from ever getting together with Chris?*

I heard footsteps and voices in the hallway downstairs. I knew what the noises meant—Chris was leaving. A few seconds later, I heard Brian go into his room and shut the door.

"Dana!"

I was so surprised, I nearly fell off my bed. It was Chris, whispering from outside my door.

"Dana! Can you hear me?"

Delighted, I scrambled off my bed and opened the door. Chris stood there, a sheepish grin on his face. I led him down the stairs.

"Hey!" I said, glad to hear Brian's stereo was far louder than our quiet voices. "I thought you left."

"I did, almost, but I came back." He paused for a moment, and I wondered if I should say something. "Follow me," he said softly.

Together, we stepped out onto the front porch.

"Anyway," he continued, "I just wanted to say good-bye. I had a really great time with you tonight."

Chris had never made a special point of saying good-bye to me before. But tonight, everything between us felt different.

"Me too."

"Except for the whole Brian thing," he added.

I rolled my eyes and sat down on the top step. "Brian can be a real hothead sometimes. He'll be okay in the morning. Besides, my social life is none of his business," I added, looking up at Chris. I wanted to reassure him that I wasn't off-limits, no matter what Brian said. I know how tight their friendship is, how loyal they are to each other, but I didn't want anything to stand in the way of what could happen between us.

"So I shouldn't paint a 'stay away' sign for you to wear around school on Monday?" he teased.

We both laughed quietly, and Chris scrunched his body next to mine on the narrow front steps. He smelled lemony and clean.

"And no billboards either, thanks," I said.

"You're not going to listen to him?" Chris asked. His voice took on a serious tone that changed the feel of the conversation.

"You mean, follow his orders?" I rolled my eyes.

Chris nodded.

"It depends on the situation, I suppose."

"In what sense?"

"Well," I said slowly, "if I meet someone and we like each other and he happens to be one of Brian's friends and a senior, then I'll just have to deal with it."

"Deal with it?" Chris prodded.

"Do what's best for me."

"Ah," Chris said, and then he fell silent. The crickets chirped as we sat and stared at each other.

The air felt thick. Suddenly all the nervous voices in my head vanished. Our faces were an inch apart, and even though we'd known each other for years, we had never been so physically close before. Not like this. Chris opened his mouth, as if he were about to say something. Then, abruptly, he stood up.

"So when can I see you again?" he asked, as if we didn't automatically see each other every day.

"Soon, I hope."

"Yes, definitely soon," I replied.

"Maybe tomorrow or something," he said. "I could come by for pancakes."

I smiled. "Like usual. Sure. That would be great."

Chris walked down the front steps. Without turning to look at me, he said under his breath, "Excellent."

Four

USUALLY SATURDAY MORNING means extra time to lounge around in bed, a chance to get a jump start on my homework, and a pancake breakfast with my family and Chris. He manages to wander over here just about the time my dad pours the batter on the griddle and I shuffle downstairs in my sweatpants, hungry from the smell of butter and hot bacon, only semiaware that Chris is at the kitchen table, again. After years, it's routine. But today was different.

I woke up early, energized, already counting the minutes until Chris would make his usual appearance at eleven. Obviously, I was too excited to even think about sleeping anymore. By nine, I was in the driveway practicing my free throws.

My thoughts drifted to last night. I replayed the whole evening out of sequence, highlighting the best parts—Chris and me sitting on the front stairs,

Chris seeing a special side to me, Chris convincing me I was "totally, thoroughly beautiful." Dazed and happy, I missed eleven free throws in a row before one went through the net.

"Nice shot."

Startled, I turned around. Chris was leaning against the big tree by the driveway, watching me.

"I didn't hear you drive up." I'd been listening for the low rumble of his dad's old Honda, hoping he might come by early.

"My dad's changing the oil. I walked."

Chris and I are not exactly neighbors—he lives at least two miles away. He must have really wanted to see me, I thought. On the other hand, he might really have had a craving for my dad's pancakes.

"How long have you been standing there?" I asked.

"Long enough to see that you need a lot of practice shooting free throws!"

"You're not kidding." I'm good on defense, but free throws have always been my weakness.

"The problem is in the way you stand," he said, coming toward me.

"What do you mean?"

"You're standing in a scoring position with your legs too far apart." He stood next to me and demonstrated with his own body. "Look," he continued. "See how my legs are? Try that."

I adjusted my feet and stood there, feeling clumsy.

"Nope," he said. He picked my right leg off the

47

ground by the heel and moved my foot toward the proper position. "Now move your other leg about eight inches apart from this one," he instructed me.

"You sure about this?" I asked. He was still holding my right leg off the ground.

"Yeah, yeah, move your left leg here, where my hand is."

"Okay, you asked for it," I said. I lifted my left leg off the ground and fell over on his back.

"Yikes—Dana!" He laughed. "You need at least *one* foot on the ground!"

"You had my right leg in the air, and you told me—"

We rolled onto the ground and ended up sort of tangled in each other. Chris freed himself, pushed against my hips, and stood up.

"I know what I said. You should listen to what I *mean*, not what I say." He grabbed my hands and pulled me up so hard that I slammed into his chest.

I tried to break away, but Chris held me firmly in place. I didn't fight it.

"Mmm. Now that's nice," he said, holding me still for a moment. My heart must have been beating a mile a minute. I was sure Chris could feel it.

Then he broke away from me, grabbed the ball, and scored.

I raced after him, but no matter how hard I tried to get control of the ball, Chris was always one step ahead of me. I'm usually a good player, but my thoughts weren't exactly on the game. And on top of everything else, Chris was cheating. After he'd score, he would immediately grab the ball and score again, which is totally against the rules.

I stepped onto the grass and put my hands on my hips. "You're not even giving me a shot," I called out.

"Yeah, yeah, yeah," he said, effortlessly making a three-point basket.

I flailed my arms around and jumped like a cheerleader. "That's all right, that's okay, cheaters are losers anyway!" I shouted.

My cheer prompted Chris to toss the ball aside and run after me. I yelped and fell to my knees, knowing there was no way I could outrun him— not that I wanted to. Chris grabbed me in his arms and wrestled me all the way to the ground.

"Come on, Dana. Use those arm muscles. Pin me."

I did pretty well, given the fact that Chris is about fifty pounds heavier than I am. I managed to roll him over on his back and secure his left shoulder to the grass, but then he flipped out from under me and I was on my back again.

For a split second, I thought of Brian watching us from his bedroom window and my stomach churned. What would he think if he saw us like this? But the dangerous thought sped away as rapidly as it had come.

"Want a second chance?" Chris asked.

"Yes," I cried, untangling myself from his grasp. But by the count of ten, I was on the defensive again, trying not to get pinned.

"More?" he teased.

"Can't," I squeaked. He wasn't hurting me, but he was definitely stronger than I was.

Chris suddenly let me go and flopped on his back like a dead fish. "C'mon. Pin me now. I'm all yours."

"You are history!" I pounced on top of him and tried to secure his arms over his head. Once again, he pinned me in about two seconds. I couldn't stop laughing. Chris lay on top of me while we caught our breath.

"Give up?" he panted.

"Not sure." I looked into the face so close to mine. Beads of perspiration had collected above Chris's lip. He hadn't shaved that morning and already his stubble looked dark and coarse.

"Okay, I'll wait." Chris adjusted his position so that he was lying next to me with my wrists held together in his hand, my torso trapped beneath his arm. There was no way I could move.

"Okay, I give up. You win! Let me go." I laughed. He released me, and I made a mad dash for the basketball and scored. Chris lay on the ground, a smile on his face as he watched me.

"Hey—isn't it time for pancakes?" he called.

I glanced at my watch and nodded. "Let's go in."

We pounded up the front steps and I pulled open the door—just in time for my mom and dad to walk out.

"Where are you going?" I asked.

"Costco," Dad replied. "We didn't have time to shop this week!" Costco is a huge food-and-everything-else warehouse where my parents buy

50

insanely large quantities of stuff—toilet paper in packages of fifty, laundry detergent in boxes as big as the washing machine, jars of peanut butter that could feed a small village.

They drove off, leaving Chris and me standing in the driveway with our stomachs growling. We remained motionless for a moment, and then Chris grabbed the ball out from under my arm, stuck it under his shirt, and ran into the house.

"No fair—that's traveling," I yelled, running behind him.

"Traveling into the house for a snack is well within the rules," he argued. He stopped triumphantly in the kitchen. I caught up to him and tried to grab the ball out from under his shirt.

"Truce, please! I'll do anything for something to eat," he begged. "I guess pancakes are out."

I released him. He took off his sweaty T-shirt and wiped his forehead with it. This wasn't unusual. But for the first time his chest caught my attention. Broad and strong, with just the right amount of curly black hair. . . .

"You . . . uh, you've got hair on your chest," I said.

"And you're as blunt this morning as you were last night," he replied, peering into the refrigerator. Hearing him mention last night made me a little uneasy. I wondered how a new day made him feel about our ride home, our whispered exchange on the stairs. Did he remember the things he'd said? Did he mean them? Wrestling with a girl is one thing; telling her she's beautiful is another.

"What do you want to eat?" he asked.

"What is there?" I replied, trying to keep my tone casual.

"Uh, not much. No wonder your parents are going shopping." Chris continued to move things around and search for goodies in the back of the refrigerator. Out came a jar that he held up proudly. "Mayonnaise!"

"We're snacking on mayonnaise?" I chuckled. "Yummy."

"Hang on, hang on." He stuck his head back in the refrigerator and hunted some more. Then he yelled out victoriously, "Chocolate cake!"

"No way. There's cake in there?"

"There's one piece on this plate. It's mine. You can have the mayonnaise."

I made a face. "Lucky me."

"I don't have the heart." Chris got out a knife and sliced the cake in half. "We'll share."

"I don't think I can eat cake for breakfast," I said.

"Live a little," Chris told me, tearing off a bite of cake and waving it beneath my nose. "Smells good, right? Think of it as a three-dimensional pancake."

"Oh, all right. I'll eat cake," I said, taking the bite in my mouth.

"Besides, this is just an appetizer. After you finish, we can go out for pizza!" He wiped a cake crumb off my face.

"I can't," I told him. "I have a study group."

"Well, what are you doing tonight? I hear Aaron's free."

"Funny." I gave him a poke in the ribs. "I'll go out with Aaron, if you'll come pick me up when we're done."

"Last night turned into a lucky night for both of us, didn't it?" Chris mused. "I guess two lucky nights in a row would be out of control, huh?"

I held my breath. Was this Chris's way of asking me out?

"Well, I'll swing by later on," he finished. Then, to my dismay, I heard Brian's feet thump down the stairs.

"My study group is coming here in an hour. We should be finished way before dinner," I encouraged him. Would he think I was being too aggressive?

Brian shuffled into the kitchen half asleep and in his sweats. "Who's coming here? And where's Dad?"

"Kim and a bunch of girls from my history class," I said shortly. I wasn't ready to forgive him for last night. "Dad's at the store, so no pancakes."

He yawned. "Hey, Chris, what's up?"

"Cake," Chris replied, leaving most of his portion on the plate. He pulled his T-shirt over his head. "Want some? I'm done."

Brian opted for cereal. Nobody said a word about last night's ordeal, and the silence hung oppressively in the air. I felt bad that Chris had seen Brian and me fighting, but Brian didn't seem to notice anything wrong. He had probably pushed it all aside by now, filling his mind with thoughts of

53

today's Braves game and an unplanned Saturday night.

"Okay, well, later," Chris said after a minute of silence.

I got up and poured myself a glass of juice. "You're leaving?" My heart was beating fast.

"I should go," he explained, heading toward the door. "Rain check on the pizza?"

"Yeah, whenever," I said as casually as possible, even though I could feel the disappointment lodge itself in my stomach. But I couldn't let it show. I couldn't let Brian catch a glimpse of what I was feeling about Chris.

"Finally," Kim said, flopping on my bed and hugging her knees to her chest in anticipation. "I'm going crazy! So, tell me. What happened last night?"

The study group had run late. Everyone but Kim had just gone home. As soon as we bid good-bye to the last member, she grabbed my hand and we scurried upstairs to my room, slamming the door behind us.

"You're not going to believe it," I said. "I've been dying to talk to you."

"I called you when I got home from work and Brian said you were still out with Aaron."

"Well . . . sort of. That's the least of it," I replied.

She raised a suspicious eyebrow. "What does *that* mean?" she said in a this–better–be–good tone.

I took a deep breath and leaned back on my elbows. "Aaron was a jerk—"

"This we know," she interrupted, tousling her hair and straightening her back. Dancers adjust their posture constantly. "Why does your brother hang out with him?"

"Aaron kind of tags along and Brian hasn't had the heart to tell him to get lost," I explained. "But *that's* definitely going to change after last night."

"Go on." Kim tilted her head in anticipation. "Tell me everything."

Just then I heard the front door open and close. Chris's voice floated upstairs. He was back!

"Dana?" Kim snapped her fingers. "Are you with me?"

My cheeks grew hot. How do you describe a feeling you get when someone you've known all your life turns into someone you barely know at all? I wasn't sure how to explain what was going on. Chris had flirted with me. He'd told me I was beautiful. He'd teased and tackled me and pinned me to the ground. Chris had wrestled with me before, of course, but suddenly everything was different. It was like being with a brand-new person. All the familiarity was washed away.

"Well," I began, "Aaron picked me up and we went to Houston's."

"Houston's?"

I nodded grimly. "He had some delusion that we were on a date. And then he had a couple of beers."

"Lovely." Kim shook her head in disgust.

I tucked my hair behind my ears. "Yeah. Well, luckily Chris saw us and drove me home." I checked for Kim's reaction, but her face remained neutral.

"And . . . ," Kim prompted eagerly.

"And, well, Chris is a big flirt."

She leaned back on my headboard. "Not exactly news, Lipton," she said.

I felt a little stupid. She was right. Maybe there was nothing uncommon happening after all.

"Brian got all upset that Aaron was a jerk," I added.

"Brian's a hothead," Kim pronounced. "But a lovable one."

"I don't know about that," I said gruffly. "He made this ludicrous rule that all his friends—which is practically the entire senior class—are off-limits to me."

Kim's mouth dropped open. "Brian passed a family law stating you can't date his friends?" she cried.

I nodded. "In front of Chris."

"What a jerk!" she said. "Does he realize that means *he* can't date your friends?"

"I didn't ask, I was so mad. All I know is . . ." I stared at the messy desk in front of me so that Kim couldn't see my eyes. ". . . this new policy of his might be kind of hard for me to follow."

Kim grinned. "I knew you liked Chris!" She laughed. "Well, who doesn't have a little crush on Chris, except me?"

I stood up and began organizing the papers on my desk.

"I mean," she went on, "Chris is totally crushable."

"Totally," I agreed, gathering my index cards into a neat pile. I glanced at Kim, who was now lying flat on her back staring at my star-covered ceiling.

"So did he kiss you?" she asked abruptly.

I spun around, shocked.

"What? No!"

"He will," she said knowingly.

"Do you know something I don't know?" I asked hopefully.

"Nothing specific." She raised her arm and outlined a constellation with her index finger. "But I have a premonition. You know how on all those talk shows the wife says she could tell the husband was having an affair, even though there was no evidence to prove it? And then the husband confesses and the wife was right all along."

"Uh-huh." Kim and I had spent many days last summer watching miserable people share their stories on bad daytime television.

"Sometimes, you just know things," Kim explained. "Sometimes, there's something in the air. And lately, something is different in the air around you and Chris. I've told you this."

If Kim could sense it, it had to be true. But that didn't mean anything would ever happen between us. Chris was practically a member of the family.

He'd never do anything to jeopardize his friendship with Brian. We might have feelings for each other, but that didn't guarantee anything would change.

"We'll see what happens tonight," Kim declared. "We'll go to Jenny Baker's party. Let's invite the guys."

It was a good idea. We'd spent lots of Saturday nights with Brian and Chris. It wouldn't seem like I was asking him to do anything out of the ordinary.

"Yeah, and?"

"And I'll make a graceful exit, leaving you time to be alone with Chris."

"What about Brian?"

Kim stood up and checked her lush hair in the mirror over my dresser.

"Leave everything to me," she said. "And keep the faith."

What else could I do? Faith was all I had to count on.

Five

MUSIC SWELLED OUT of Jenny Baker's open front door. Dozens of kids lingered on the lawn—it looked as if the entire sophomore class had decided to spend the evening at her party. Unlike the scene at Houston's, there were no seniors as far as I could tell. As soon as we got inside, Brian and Chris shrugged at each other, scanning unfamiliar faces for people they might know.

"Come on, Brian, I'll introduce you to some people," Kim said, leading him through the haze of cigarette smoke and mounds of cracked plastic drinking cups. I chewed my lip. Her plan to get me alone with Chris was already underway. Chris shifted his weight from one leg to the other.

"Are you bored?" I asked nervously.

He smiled down at me. "You're here, so how could I possibly be bored?"

I fought back the excitement bubbling up inside

me. "Well, um, what I mean is . . . you don't really know anyone."

"Doesn't matter," he reassured me. "I know you. I know Brian and Kim. I know that Jenny Baker has a lot of money to live in a house like this." Chris gazed around the room in awe.

Who could blame him? The house looked more like a landmark Southern mansion than a place where ordinary people lived. The stairs were wide and majestic, and the antique wood banister was massive enough to support the dozen or so kids draped over it. The entrance foyer was twice the size of my bedroom, and the living room had been roped off, probably to prevent careless partyers from spilling things on the ornate furniture. Most people were out in the backyard, by the lap-length swimming pool. Jenny Baker was definitely from old money. Chris and I were not.

"Doesn't look a lot like my house," I said, picking up a hand-painted porcelain candy bowl filled with creased cigarette butts. My house was like every other house on the block—two stories, three trees, garage off to the side, beige paint. Even the grass grew at the same rate as our neighbors'.

Chris grimaced. "Looks *nothing* like my house." I'd never been to Chris's house, but Brian once told me it looked pretty dilapidated, as if his parents didn't care about where they lived.

"No wonder Jenny's so spoiled. She must get everything she wants," I said, remembering the time Jenny Baker sobbed hysterically when she didn't make the track team. She'd acted as if it were the biggest catastrophe of her life. *Maybe if she'd practiced running around her living room, she'd have done better at tryouts,* I thought wryly.

"I'll bet she does," Chris agreed.

"Well, I'm not impressed by gaudy houses," I said.

"Me neither." Chris cheered up suddenly. He pointed to the wave of new partyers headed toward the pool. "Let's go."

Outside, the patio served as an excellent dance floor. Chris guided me toward a bunch of people dancing in large groups. "Dance with me," he said.

I have to admit that Chris is sort of a goofy dancer. I mean, he's really coordinated on the playing field, but on the dance floor he shuffles from one foot to the other and that's about it. I didn't mind. I thought he looked sweet. I guess that's what happens when you really like someone—even when he acts goofy you think he looks sweet.

"You're an awesome dancer," Chris said, grabbing my hands and swinging them in the air.

"You just have to feel the beat," I told him, "and not really think about it." Gripping his hands, I tried to show Chris how to move. It was no use.

Someone changed the CD to a slow song, and Chris pulled me close. We swayed from side to side for a little while, our faces close enough for me to smell his shampoo. I'd never really slow danced with anyone before. In junior high, the minute the deejay played a song without a fast beat, all the guys scattered to the end of the room and kidded around with each other while the girls ran to the bathroom to hide. Even now someone yelled, "Change the music," but Chris's grasp remained firm. He was definitely unwilling to let go. *What would Brian think if he saw us?* I thought nervously, my palms beginning to sweat. I prayed he wouldn't.

When the song was over, a girl from my bio class tapped me on the shoulder.

"Hey, Debbie," I said. I couldn't remember her last name. Some people's first and last names are inseparably connected, like Jenny Baker or Joanna Winterson. Then there are others, like Kim and me and Chris and this girl Debbie, whose last names are usually completely ignored.

"Hey, Dana, hey . . ."

"This is Chris," I told her.

"Are you a friend of Jenny Baker's?" Debbie asked Chris.

"Never met her," Chris said. "I'm with Dana."

Debbie winked. "Oh. Sorry. I didn't mean to interrupt."

"No problem," Chris said. "Nice to meet you."

"You too," Debbie said. "Way to go, Dana," she whispered in my ear as she melted back into the party crowd.

"Way to go, Dana?" Chris repeated as he pulled me close for another slow dance. His eyes twinkled.

"Is that what she said? I could barely hear her," I lied. Of course Chris and I looked like a couple—he hadn't left my side since we'd arrived. The thought made me smile . . . but then Brian's rule flashed in my mind. As long as *Brian* didn't think we looked like a couple, everything would be great.

Someone finally got fed up with slow dancing, because the music suddenly went dead. Chris let go of me and we stood there awkwardly waiting for another song to take its place. After a few futile attempts to find a good radio station, someone put on a Stone Temple Pilots CD and about thirty yelping people hurled themselves toward the dance area.

Just then, Kim and Brian came up to us. They were soaking wet.

"What happened to you?" I asked. Kim's strawberry-blond hair was plastered to her cheeks and my brother's tan shirt was transparent.

"Pool fight," Kim said through gritted teeth. "Some jerk got hold of a huge trash can and doused everyone with water." She rubbed her eyes. "And the chlorine stings!"

"We lost the fight," Brian added, wringing out a soggy pant leg. His eyes roved disdainfully over the crowd. "Sophomores." He shook his head. "Let's get out of here."

I wasn't eager to leave the party and Kim knew it, but Brian had already started to push his way through the crowd. Chris followed him. Kim and I walked a step behind the guys, back into the house, past the dazzling staircase, and through the foyer.

Debbie was sitting on the staircase with another girl. She caught my eye as we walked past. "Bye, you guys! You make a cute couple," she called. Chris waved at her.

"You sure do!" Kim whispered to me.

"Do you think Brian heard that?" I cried.

Kim shot a glance at my brother, who was already halfway out the door, still wringing his shirt.

"Not a chance," she assured me. She hurried ahead of Chris. "I get the front seat!"

As soon as we all piled into the car, Brian drove off in a hurry. He was shivering in his wet clothes. Kim rubbed her arms while they exchanged *brrr* sounds.

Chris stretched out in the backseat with his head in my lap. I looked down at him in shock. I mean, Brian was right in front of us! All he had to do was look in the rearview mirror and . . .

I closed my eyes for a moment and concentrated on how wonderful it felt to have Chris touch me—on the basketball court, on the dance floor, in the car. If Chris had the guts to put his head in my lap, I would have the guts to enjoy it.

Brian's and Kim's chlorine-saturated clothes infused the air with an antiseptic odor. It reminded me of being in the hospital, with its chemical-clean smell. Sterile and cold and anonymous. Sitting here with Chris, I could barely remember how alone and frightened I'd been in those days.

I rested my hands on Chris's head and felt his velvety dark hair. He rolled over so that his face was toward the roof of the car and moved my hands so that they covered his eyes.

"Tired?" I asked.

"Yeah."

"Better than freezing," Brian said, sneaking a peek at us in the rearview mirror.

Yikes.

"True," Chris agreed, yawning again.

Brian shot us a second glance as he pulled onto the highway. I looked out the window at the dark night and pretended not to notice Brian noticing us. Cars whizzed by in the opposite direction, blurring my view of the city. Their low roar almost hypnotized me.

I imagined Chris would come back to my house that night and hang out for a while like he usually did. We could watch a movie and make popcorn, or sit around and talk about nothing, waiting for Brian to go upstairs to bed. Anything—I didn't care what we did. I just wanted to stay near him.

Chris rolled his head around, jolting me from my roaming thoughts.

"Why are you so tired?" I asked.

"You wore me out. Basketball. Dancing. I'm pooped." His voice trailed off and he pretended to snore.

"Mmm, that's attractive," Kim remarked. Brian shot another look in the rearview mirror.

Then Chris stopped, and the four of us got very quiet. It was as if each of us were waiting for something to happen, but none of us knew what.

Brian glanced in the mirror again. "What's going on back there anyway?" he said.

To my dismay, Chris sat up and moved closer to his side of the car. "Not much, man. I'm beat."

I shifted in my seat. Why did Brian have to go and ruin everything?

"I'm calling it a night," Chris said. "Drop Kim off first since she's wet, and then swing by my place." Kim stretched her arm along the back of the front passenger seat and waved her pinkie at me.

We reached Kim's house about two minutes later.

"I'll call you tomorrow," she told me, wiggling her eyebrows. I laughed.

Chris got out and took Kim's place up front. For the rest of the drive to his house, he didn't say a word to me or Brian.

Please turn around, I willed silently. *Please let me know you're just as upset as I am.*

He didn't. A moment later we pulled into his driveway. What a sharp contrast to Jenny Baker's place—Chris's house was pretty run-down. It looked as if it hadn't been painted in years. Clearly, no one had cut the grass in months. Even in the dark I could make out an old electric saw and a few miscellaneous bicycle parts littering the driveway and the lawn. Chris must have known I was checking out his house. I hoped he wasn't embarrassed, but I could see that he was frowning.

"See ya," he muttered, getting out of the car.

"Later," Brian said.

"See ya," I echoed, hoping for something more. But without turning to look at me, Chris ran to his front door, unlocked it, and disappeared inside.

Brian and I drove home in silence.

Six

MONDAY WAS COLUMBUS DAY, a school holiday. A big rainstorm had flooded the driveway, so I couldn't practice my free throws. With Kim at work, and without a driver's license, my afternoon promised to be both housebound and boring.

At about five o'clock, Brian fell asleep in front of *Jurassic Park*. I continued to watch, even though I'd seen the movie at least five times.

"Hello? Anybody home?"

I nearly jumped out of my seat.

I scurried to the front hall. There was Chris, his eyes glinting, smile wide.

"Shhh. Brian's asleep," I whispered, putting my finger on my lips.

"No problem," he whispered back, neatly hanging his rain jacket on the coatrack and heading toward the den.

Brian raised his head about a half inch off the couch. "Hey," he muttered.

Chris grinned at me. "I'll bet he's asleep for the night."

"I heard that," Brian mumbled. Half his mouth was squished on the pillow, making his sharp angular face look like a pile of Play-Doh. "And it's not true."

Chris and I exchanged glances. Then we both sat down and watched Brian. Within about two minutes, he was out cold. Chris motioned for me to accompany him to the kitchen.

"We should whisper," I said, hoisting myself up on the counter.

"Okay."

"I'll bet he does sleep through the night," I said, checking the digital clock on the microwave. "I know it's only a little after five, but he's done it before."

With my parents running errands and Brian sacked out in the den, Chris and I were basically alone.

I'd never worried about making conversation with Chris. Everything always had been so natural between us. But now . . . now things were different. At least they *felt* different. Or maybe I was the one who felt different.

"So," I said finally.

"So."

"So, uh, do you want anything?"

"Do I want anything?" he repeated.

"Yeah, like, uh, something to drink? Or eat? Or something? We're out of chocolate cake. How about some mayonnaise," I teased. I drummed my fingers on the counter, wishing I didn't feel so nervous.

"No, no food. How about a back rub?"

"You want a *back rub?*" My voice almost squeaked. Was this the same Chris who wouldn't even look at me in Brian's car?

"Yeah. Do you mind?"

Of course I didn't mind. "No, that's fine," I said, trying to sound casual.

Sitting on the kitchen counter put me in the perfect position. Chris turned away from me and I gently gripped his shoulders.

I worked my way down his spine, stopping when I reached his hips, then ran my fingernails up to his neck and massaged his head. We'd never given each other a back rub before, and I knew that if Brian came into the kitchen and saw us, he would freak out. The thought of being caught scared and excited me at the same time.

I continued for about fifteen minutes. Then I stopped and gently patted Chris's head. "All done," I said. "Better?"

"Much better. You can't imagine," he said, turning around to face me. Chris is about five inches taller than me, but sitting on the counter brought our faces to the same height. We were as close to each other as when we slow danced at Jenny Baker's party.

Chris put his hands on my shoulders. Then he started

to gently squeeze my arms, working his way down to my hands. He looked in my eyes the entire time.

"You're all tensed up," he said. "I'll help you relax." He reached around and gently rubbed the back of my neck, never taking his eyes from mine. I was so nervous, I was afraid I might yelp.

I held my breath as Chris gently inched his body closer to mine. He stopped massaging my neck and held both of my hands in his, gently rubbing them with his thumbs.

"Thanks for the back rub," he said softly.

"You too," I answered stupidly, waiting for whatever would happen next. A kiss, most likely. I certainly wouldn't have minded that. I'd kissed two other guys before—one in a truth or dare game, the other at a New Year's Eve party. Neither was memorable, except that the first one certified me as someone who'd been kissed, and the second one showed me what it was like to be kissed badly. Kissing Chris would be unlike anything I'd ever experienced. I knew it would be wonderful.

He leaned closer.

"Hey—where'd everybody go?" Brian called out from the den.

Chris held me for a second—and then he let go.

"We're in the kitchen," he answered, releasing my hands and taking a step backward. "I'm on my way home," he added.

"You just got here," Brian complained.

"I only stopped by to say hi," Chris replied. He

smiled at me. "Close one," he whispered, his face revealing a combination of relief and frustration.

"Mmm-hmm." Disappointed, I lowered myself off the counter and headed for the den to join my brother. What would have happened next? I could imagine, but I'd never know.

From behind me, I heard Chris say, "We'll definitely have to try that again."

Kim called after eleven o'clock and my parents weren't pleased. I begged them to let me talk for five precious minutes. They relented, and I took the call in my room.

"Okay, you're definitely right," I said hurriedly. "Your hunches were on—there's no way Chris is just flirting with me. It can't be."

"Fantastic," Kim said. "When's the wedding?"

"Ha! We're a long way from that. There are a few obstacles."

"Such as?"

"First of all, I know Chris says nice things about me, but I've always been like a little sister to him. Should I believe the things he's saying now? On the other hand, there's no reason he'd go for someone younger and less experienced unless he really liked me, right? I mean, *you'd* never go for your little brother's friends. . . ."

"In case you haven't noticed, Dana, my brother's friends are nine," Kim cracked.

"But if they weren't," I protested.

"I'm not going for a nine-year-old, that's true,

71

but you and Chris are a totally different thing."

"Convince me."

"You're into the same sports. . . ."

"We like the same music," I interrupted, encouraged.

"Excellent," she said eagerly.

"We know each other really well," I went on. Then I thought of all I didn't know about Chris—like his family life, why his house was such a mess, the details of his many romances. "Sort of," I added dejectedly.

"You're comfortable with each other," Kim reminded me.

"Very. But there's another problem," I told her.

"All problems can be solved."

I don't know what I'd do without Kim. "Not Brian's off-limits rule."

Kim hesitated. "You can't be off-limits to an entire grade."

"I know. But Brian doesn't see it that way. And I'm *definitely* off-limits to Chris, as far as he and Brian are concerned."

Kim sighed dramatically. "Dana, you can't live by someone else's rules. You just have to let things happen naturally between you and Chris and deal with the results as they come up."

"I know," I said sadly. "I just hope Chris knows it too." I thought about how Chris had grown silent in the car on Saturday night. But then today he gave me a neck rub. *He's obviously as mixed-up as I am*, I thought. *Chris might flirt with me for the rest of our lives and never really do anything about it.*

"That's the wait-and-see test, Dana," she said. "There's nothing much you can do."

"Isn't it weird," I mused, "how one day you think of a guy as one thing, like an older brother, and then the next day he's someone else entirely, like someone you could really fall in love with."

"Yeah, well, you know. I think I know exactly what you mean," Kim said. She paused. "Actually, speaking of that—"

My call waiting beeped. "Hang on," I told Kim. I pressed the on/off button to switch calls.

It was Chris.

"Hey," I said, flustered.

"Hey, it's you. Lucky me," Chris said.

"Hang on a sec. I'll get off the other line so that you can talk to Brian." I switched back to Kim, told her it was Chris, and cut off our connection. Then I switched back to Chris. "I'll get Brian." I started to put the phone down.

"No wait—Dana? Dana?"

I put the receiver back to my ear. "Uh-huh?"

"Get this," he said, excited. "The Scorching Stones have a new CD coming out next month. I just found out."

"Excellent!" I said. "I can't wait to get it."

"Are you going to hear them on Saturday?"

I didn't know what he was talking about. "Scorching Stones? Are they playing?"

"They're giving a free concert at the amphitheater."

"Wow, the rumor's true! Are you going?" I asked.

73

"Yeah, and you should come with me. It's going to be an awesome show."

"I'd love it," I told him. "Maybe Brian will drive," I added automatically. I could have kicked myself.

"Brian hates the Scorching Stones," Chris pointed out. "There's no way he'll want to go."

"That's right, he does," I said. "He would just sit and complain about how bad they are." I paused. Brian might not want to join us, but did that mean we should keep our plan a secret? "I guess we'll tell him we're going," I said doubtfully. "Right?"

"Yeah, sure, of course," Chris replied quickly. "We can always hook up with him after the concert. You know, if we want. So, you're coming?"

I swallowed. It wasn't as if Chris had never asked me to do anything . . . like the time he invited me to the amusement park because rides make Brian sick to his stomach, or the night we went to the college basketball semifinals because Brian was cramming for an exam. Maybe I shouldn't read anything into Chris's offer now—it seemed like a totally casual invitation. Maybe he just wanted to hear a concert with a friend. But in my heart, I knew this invitation was different. I could feel it.

And I wasn't about to miss a chance at being alone with Chris—no matter what Brian said.

What if it were the beginning of *us?* What if Saturday night changed everything?

"I'll go with you," I told him. "Definitely."

Seven

"EXCITED?" CHRIS ASKED on Saturday night. I had just climbed into his car.

I could only nod. *Excited* wasn't the word to describe what I was feeling.

"What's Brian doing?" Chris asked casually. "You told him we're going, right?"

I nodded, trying to act as if I didn't care what Brian thought about this whole thing. "He didn't want to come. He's going to the movies with Peter and Jamie."

When I'd asked Brian if he wanted to come, he'd just snorted and shook his head. "You two go get scorched. You couldn't *pay* me to go."

I was pretty sure Brian didn't suspect anything. I'd tried not to be too obvious, but I wanted to look at least a little special. I had on my favorite jeans and a tight velvet top, and my hair was down instead of up in my usual ponytail. I'd even worn a little mascara and lipstick—unusual for me—but Brian was too busy checking the movie times to notice.

During the concert, Chris and I clapped and sang and shouted like everyone else. We were having such a good time, I almost forgot there was something . . . different about us now. *Almost.*

Afterward, we got into Chris's car and snaked our way out of the crowded parking lot. The concert had left both of us exhilarated and totally starved. The night was warm, so we picked up sandwiches from Publix and ate on a bench by the lake in Chastain Park.

I inhaled my turkey with Swiss on rye before Chris had finished half of his ham and American cheese on white.

"Slow down, tiger," he laughed. "You'll choke."

I smiled and cupped my hand over my neck as I swallowed hard.

"I never noticed . . . you have freckles on the base of your neck," he said as I removed my hand. He reached out to touch them.

I laughed nervously. "Sort of." In the lamplight, the little reddish brown bumps must have looked iridescent. Chris's finger traced a path from one to the next. I gently moved his hand away.

"Sort of? What does that mean?" he asked, tilting his head to the side to try to see the marks beneath my chin.

"They're scars," I explained. "From all the needles and stuff."

"You mean from when you—" Chris stopped, looking embarrassed. People are afraid to say the word *cancer* to someone who's had it, as if saying it will lead to something grim. I got over that superstition a long time ago.

"From when I had leukemia," I finished for him. "Cancer."

"Right, I know," he said. "I just wasn't sure you'd want to talk about it."

"I don't mind." It's true I hardly ever talk about my illness. But that's because no one ever asks. Not even Kim.

"So, tell me about it," Chris said, looking closely at me.

"Tell you about it? Like, what I did when I found out I had cancer? Or what it was like?"

"Yeah. Tell me anything. Tell me everything," he said, putting his hand gently on my knee. It made me feel safe. Important. Glad that finally someone wanted me to talk about what it was like to be sick.

"I don't know where to start," I admitted. "Nobody expected I had anything as serious as leukemia. My parents thought I had mono or pneumonia or some ordinary disease most kids get. So, my mom took me to the doctor and he gave me a blood test and a chest X ray, and the results weren't good. A few days later, we learned the truth, that I had cancer. I was only seven. I was really too young to understand what it all meant."

"What did your parents tell you?" Chris asked softly.

"My mother told me I was going to be sick for a while, but that if I made myself a promise to get better, I would," I said. Chris nodded. "I believed her. I didn't know anything about chemotherapy or radiation—or dying. All I knew was that I felt awful pretty much all the time and couldn't wait to go home from the hospital."

"The hospital was really bad, huh?"

I shook my head. "It wasn't really *bad* . . . it was just strange. The staff did everything they could to make the whole experience pleasant—or at least bearable. I was in a children's ward. The walls were painted with zoo animals and circus tents and balloons. The nurses were really friendly, and they'd bring in special guests to make us feel better, like clowns and singers and jugglers."

"Sounds almost fun," Chris said, taking my hand. "But it couldn't have been fun at all."

"Well, sometimes that part was fun," I admitted. "But somehow I always knew that the adults were smiling and laughing too hard, like they were trying to make us forget we were in a cancer ward." I smiled sadly as I remembered. "All the mothers had red swollen eyes as if they'd been crying forever. And all the fathers were rigid and uptight, like they were trying *not* to cry. You know what I mean—everyone was a little *too* happy when the puppeteer came."

"It felt forced?"

"Yeah," I said. I had never told anyone, not even my parents, that I'd been able to see the pain behind everyone's smiles. "At least I thought it felt forced, and I'm sure some of the older kids thought so too. But I think the younger kids enjoyed everything."

"Tell me more," Chris said. "What were some of the scary parts?"

Unexpectedly, I felt tears sting my eyes. It had been so long since I'd thought of those months, let alone spoken of them. But something about Chris made me want to speak, to share my memories with him. I took a deep breath.

"Well, some things were really terrifying. Some kids were in so much pain they couldn't sleep. They just lay awake all night, screaming. That was frightening, hearing them, knowing you might be in pain someday too. Knowing you couldn't make them stop crying."

"*Were* you ever in pain?" Chris whispered.

"No, not really. For me, it was mostly this horrible feeling of weakness all the time. Some things did hurt for a little while, like when the doctors had to use big needles for certain tests. . . ." I wiped away a tear. "You probably don't want to hear about that part."

Chris squeezed my hand. "I want to hear anything you want to tell me," he said sincerely. "You can't say anything wrong or stupid or embarrassing. You understand that, right? You're totally safe with me."

Suddenly, I felt a tremendous release. I'd spent so much energy trying to put my illness behind me and live a normal life. I was tired of *not* thinking about it, *not* talking about it. When Chris said that I could tell him anything, I felt as if I'd never stop.

"There was one horrendous night," I told him, "when I thought I wouldn't make it to the morning. I didn't really understand that I was dying or anything like that, but I felt so unbearably sick. . . . I can't even explain it. I was so weak I couldn't even roll over in bed. I barely had enough energy to breathe or open my eyes. I had gone through a bone marrow transplant about a week before."

"What is that, exactly?" Chris asked. "I've seen ads on TV asking people to become bone marrow donors."

"That's when they take out all your bone marrow and replace it with healthy marrow from someone else," I explained. "It's complicated because the marrow has to match perfectly. A lot of times no one in the family is a suitable match. That's what happened with me. My parents couldn't be donors, and even Brian's marrow wasn't the right match. I was incredibly lucky. I got a matching donor from the national registry."

"Who gave you their marrow?" Chris asked.

"It's all done anonymously, so I'll never know. Someone volunteered and added her—or his—name to the donor registry, and eventually became my marrow donor." I looked out at the lake, still and shining in the glow of the streetlights and the moon.

"I owe that person my life, that's for sure. I hope that somehow he or she knows how grateful I am." I smiled and turned back to Chris. "When I was better, I drew a thank-you picture and my doctors promised they'd send it to the donor through the registry. I'm not sure whether my donor ever got it."

Chris looked impressed. "That's amazing. A stranger, an ordinary person, volunteered to give their bone marrow to someone with cancer."

"It is incredible," I agreed. "I'd donate my marrow, but I'm not allowed. I can't donate blood either, just in case there are still traces of cancer."

"Did the transplant hurt?" Chris asked.

"Not really. Basically, you just sit there and the stuff trickles in through an IV. But when it was all done, I had to stay in isolation for eight weeks. See, you're really susceptible to infection after a bone marrow transplant, because it totally wipes out your immune system. The smallest germ or piece of dirt can, well . . . kill you."

"Oh, geez." Chris rubbed my arm sympathetically.

"I was in a special room with a plastic shield separating me from my family. No one could touch me. We could see and hear each other, but except for when the doctors came to check on me, I was by myself."

Chris's eyes showed me his concern was real.

"So, that's when you thought you wouldn't make it?" he asked.

I looked up at the sky and breathed in the beautiful night air. How lucky I was to be alive. "One of those nights, I got a raging fever. It was some terrible infection. My parents had gone out in the hall to talk to the doctor, I think. But Brian was there—he spent every night of those eight weeks at the hospital with me. He sat on the other side of the shield and read me stories and played me tapes and told me about what he had done that day." I laughed. "He always used to insist to my parents that he wasn't tired. So they'd let him stay, and then he'd fall asleep on the folding chair. One night, he actually fell off!"

Chris smiled too. "I can't believe your parents let him spend so much time there."

"Well, I guess they didn't really *let* him. Brian kind of refused to leave. He just wouldn't go. I remember him throwing an unbelievable fit one day. And after that, no one had any problem letting him hang out. Plus, it was during the summer, so he didn't have to go to school in the morning. My parents figured if he was that serious about not leaving me, it would be better just to let him stay. It was against hospital rules, but the doctors and nurses pretended not to notice."

"Brian always was stubborn!" Chris chuckled. "Go on. What happened the night you had the fever?"

I paused for a moment. "Chris," I said, "nobody knows what I'm about to tell you, okay?"

"It's not like I'm going to talk about it in school or anything," he assured me.

"No, I mean, even Brian doesn't know that I know what I'm going to tell you," I said.

"Okay." Chris took my hand. "Whatever you tell me stops with me. I promise, no matter what."

"Okay," I whispered. I knew I might burst into

tears at any second, but I was already in too deep. I really wanted Chris to know everything. Somehow, I knew he would still care about me no matter what I told him.

"The night I thought I wasn't going to make it," I began, "Brian was there, sitting in that folding chair. He was awake. He must have thought I was sleeping. I mean, I'm sure I looked like I was asleep. I couldn't open my eyes more than a tiny crack. I couldn't *move*." I sighed. "Anyway, Brian started to talk to himself. He was crying, quietly but sort of . . . violently. Somehow, even though I was so sick, I knew he was getting hysterical. But I couldn't say or do anything."

Chris nodded.

"And then he started to pray," I continued. "He said he was sorry for anything bad he'd ever done. He listed all the things he felt guilty about, like cheating on his spelling test and taking home a baseball from the Y by accident, and yelling at me when I took stuff from his room. He said he was sorry for all the times he'd eaten my dessert and said mean things to me or told me to drop dead."

I shivered and pulled my jacket close around me. Chris put his arm around my shoulders to warm me up.

"I mean, Brian was only a kid too," I added. "Kids say all sorts of mean stuff to each other, especially brothers and sisters. But Brian felt really bad. He swore that if I got better, he'd take good care of me forever. He kept saying that over and over again, until finally he fell asleep."

"And you did get better," Chris stated.

"The transplant worked, and I got healthier and healthier. I was out of the hospital by Labor Day, just in time for my eighth birthday. After about six months I went into remission, which means there were no signs of the cancer in my body. Then, after five years of remission, the doctors told me I was cured."

"So that's why Brian is so overprotective," Chris said slowly. "Because of everything that happened."

"Right. Because he's afraid something bad will happen to me again, and because he made this deal with himself to always take care of me." I wiped the tears off my face and smiled. "He does take awfully good care of me."

"Yes, he does," Chris agreed, catching a tear from my chin with the back of his hand. "He loves you like crazy."

"I'm lucky to have him," I said. "But I try so hard to live every day to the fullest. I do everything I can to stay healthy and be brave. Sometimes, Brian's being so overprotective squashes my energy a little. It's hard. I don't want to hurt his feelings. . . ."

"No, but at the same time you have to have your own life."

"Exactly." How had Chris gotten to be such a good listener? And when had he become my closest friend?

I could feel the last few tears drying on my cheeks. Chris took my hand again and led me from the bench to the soft grass. We sat close, side-by-side, and Chris wrapped both of his arms around me. For a few minutes, he stroked my hair and held my head with his hand. I felt perfectly relaxed.

Then Chris turned my face toward his. He looked deeply into my eyes as he gently smoothed a tear from my cheek. And then his lips were on mine, motionless for a moment. I could feel his smooth, soft skin on my face, and then he was kissing me and I was kissing him back.

In my imagination, kissing Chris had been wonderful but awkward. In reality, kissing Chris felt as natural as talking to him. It was like a different way of talking. Totally honest, direct, and incredibly exciting.

Chris pulled away and looked at me, as if to ask whether what he'd done was okay.

"Wow," he said.

"Wow."

"Uh, well, *wow*."

I laughed.

"So, uh, I should tell you," he said. "I didn't mean for that to—wait, let me start again. Don't think that was just some cheap shot or anything."

"What do you mean?"

"Well, I didn't kiss you because you were sad or anything. I mean, I did, of course, but—" He took a deep breath. "What I'm trying to say is, I kissed you because I wanted to. Because I've been dying to kiss you for a long time, and I figured I'd better just get up enough nerve to actually do it and see what happened."

"So that was an experiment?" I teased.

"No, not at all! What I mean is—Dana, I really like you. I've never felt so strongly about anyone. Not the way I feel about you. I've known you for years as my friend's kid sister, almost like *my* kid sister . . . but it's all different now. You know what I mean?"

I nodded. "Oh yes."

"Before tonight," he said, "I never believed we'd actually, well, kiss. I never believed you'd be my—my girlfriend."

Girlfriend? Was I hearing correctly?

"Until now, you were always my big brother's friend," I said. "My other big brother."

"And you were Brian's adorable little sister. But now, you're so much more than that."

"You too," I said, holding on to his arm. The fact that Chris was older thrilled me, made me feel courageous and special and protected. And the fact that he was Chris Geller, the really nice guy who'd watched me grow up, gave me the freedom to be myself. To be the real me.

"I've been thinking about us a lot lately too," I said. "But I kind of thought we couldn't ever really be a couple."

"This has to turn into something, don't you think?" Chris urged. "We *have* to be a couple. Because the way I feel about you is so intense . . . I can't explain it, but you understand what I'm saying, right?"

Suddenly Chris frowned and pulled away from

me. "I mean, I'm not completely off the wall, am I? Please tell me I didn't just make a total fool of myself."

Instead of answering, I kissed him. I could tell he liked it. He smiled and touched my cheek, staring into my eyes as if his were telling me something significant, something extraordinary. But then, without warning, he dropped his hand and sat back.

"There is one problem," he said. "A big one."

"Brian."

"Right. He'd kill me if he knew."

"I can talk to him about that," I said quickly, grasping his hand.

"You think you can?" he asked. "I'm not sure."

"I can try."

Chris took his hand away and ran it through his hair. "Brian's going to have a totally bad reaction. He'll say I betrayed him. I guess maybe I have."

"That's not true," I argued. "Keeping your feelings a secret would have betrayed *us*. Let me try to talk to Brian."

Chris stood up. "Maybe I just did a really stupid thing," he said. "You didn't see how he yelled at Aaron the day after that night I had to drive you home. It wasn't pretty—and Aaron wasn't even a good friend. Maybe this was a bad mistake."

I stood and put my arms around him. "Kissing you felt totally right to me. Did kissing me feel that way?"

"Well, yeah, while I was doing it," he admitted.

"That's what matters. We can find a way to make Brian understand," I said.

Chris nodded slowly. "Yeah, maybe. Not right away, but sometime. I know you don't want to hurt him."

"And you don't want to be a bad friend," I said. "But didn't you just tell me I have to live my own life?"

Chris looked into my eyes, and without any more words I knew we both understood what we were getting ourselves into. This couldn't be some casual fling. Our relationship was too deep already, and there were other people's feelings to consider. Whatever was going to happen between us would definitely be risky, and it was certain to be intense. But we had come too far to turn back now.

Suddenly I felt a little nervous. Would it feel right, being with Chris all the time? Had we been friends for so long that we couldn't be anything more?

He leaned forward and kissed me gently. Then he tightened his arms around my waist and kissed me again.

What am I afraid of? I thought as I kissed him back. *Everything is exactly the way it's supposed to be.*

Eight

"SHE SHOOTS, SHE scores!" I ran out in the crisp autumn air. I smiled as the ball sailed cleanly through the hoop. It was early Sunday morning, and I was playing basketball in my driveway. I'd only been out there for ten minutes when I heard a car pull up.

"Get in," Chris called quietly from his dad's car, glancing at the house as if he didn't want to wake anyone up.

I was so happy to see him. I'd had a feeling he might drop by.

He opened the passenger door and I hopped inside. He drove to the end of the block. Then he stopped the car and kissed me.

"I missed you," he said. "So much. All night."

"Me too. I couldn't sleep." It was true. My night was filled with half-sleeping, half-waking dreams of Chris and me.

"I've been circling your house for an hour hoping you'd come outside," he said.

"No way—really?"

"Honest." Chris crossed his heart. "I wanted to scoop you up and spend the day with you before anyone else knew about it." He began to drive again and I shivered with excitement.

"Where are we going?" I asked. I had a momentary flash of guilt about taking off without leaving a note—my parents were having brunch with some friends. But I pushed it away. If Chris wanted me to escape with him, I would. Besides, my parents weren't the real problem. Brian was.

What would he do if he found out where I was . . . or who I was with?

"I'm not sure," Chris said. "We could drive down to Rabun County and look at the mountains. Maybe take a hike or something."

"Sounds good." I was sure Chris could tell I was trembling. Nervous energy bubbled up inside me until I thought I might burst. Chris looked over at me and smiled. Then he put the car in gear and drove off with one hand on the wheel, the other hand in mine.

A few miles later, Chris popped a CD into the CD player. I rolled down the window as the sound of an old Scorching Stones song blared from the speakers. The Georgia sun warmed my face and cool salty air stung my eyes. I smiled, thinking how good it felt to be healthy and alive.

We cruised down Interstate 85, passing roadside

carts full of fruit for sale and shacks with signs offering fresh hot peanuts and homemade ice cream. We drove by farms, the horses grazing in the moist grass, lifting their heads to watch the cars on the highway. I loved Georgia. I loved being in control of my free time. And I loved Chris.

Is it too soon to admit that? I wondered. *Maybe I should just not worry about it. Today I'll simply concentrate on having one of the greatest days of my life.*

The mountains in Rabun County are not very high, but buried between them are beautiful rocky paths, blustering waterfalls, and a wonderful still silence you can't find in the city. When I was in the hospital and the medication made me really sensitive to noises and smells and bright lights, I tried to picture the mountains with their soft sweet aromas and the peaceful sounds of chirping frogs and running streams. Something about it felt healing. I could hardly believe that Chris wanted to take me to the mountains now—it was almost as if he knew this was my favorite place in the world.

"Did you see Brian last night?" Chris asked, dragging me back to reality.

Brian. My invisible, uninvited chaperone.

"No," I said. "Thankfully. I wouldn't have known what to say."

"How about, 'Hey, the concert was great,'" Chris joked.

"No, silly, about us."

"You would have said something?" Chris asked, the concern in his voice obvious.

"I don't know. I don't think so—not yet anyway. Not without having talked about it with you first." I turned my head to look at Chris while he drove. I liked to watch the way his brow wrinkled as he concentrated on the road.

"What would you have told him?" Chris asked. "If you had said something."

"I don't know," I admitted. "What *should* I have told him?"

"I mean, do you generally report to him when someone kisses you?" Chris said, smiling. Just hearing him mention our kiss sent a shiver through me.

"No." I blushed. "Although it doesn't happen every day."

"Good," he said. "I wouldn't want it to. Unless it was with me."

At that moment, I couldn't imagine ever wanting to kiss anyone else.

"I'll kiss you every day, if you like," I told him.

Chris stared straight ahead, an eager grin creeping over his face.

"That," he said, "would be excellent."

After driving for about an hour, we pulled off the highway onto a dirt road. Chris turned off the ignition. "We're here."

"Great!" I answered. "Where's here?"

"My favorite place." We got out of the car and Chris took my hand. "In a few minutes you'll see why."

He led me through the bushes to a narrow hiking

trail that ended at the base of a waterfall. The blue-and-white cascades of water sparkled in the sunlight and formed a pool about thirty feet below. It was beautiful. The water made a constant roar, but the whole place felt silent and peaceful. Nobody else was around.

"How come there aren't a hundred people here?" I exclaimed. "Doesn't anyone know about this place?"

"I've never seen anyone here," Chris said, sitting down on a flat, gray rock. "You can't see the waterfall from the road, so a lot of people probably don't know it exists."

I planted myself next to him and let the cool water mist my face.

"How often do you come here?" I asked.

"Whenever I need to get away from my family and your brother isn't around." Chris gazed thoughtfully at the scenery. "I suppose I come here pretty often."

Poor Chris! I never knew he felt so troubled. He'd always been so easygoing and carefree when he was at my house. I wondered if Brian realized how much Chris depended on him for comfort.

"Chris," I said gently. "How come you spend so much time at my house and Brian hardly ever spends any time at yours?"

"That's easy," he said, holding out his hand so that he could count the reasons on his fingers. "First, you have a bigger house and a better TV."

"Okay." We do have a huge TV. It's one of my father's prized possessions.

"Second, Brian has the prettiest sister of anyone I know, so that's always an extra perk."

I smiled. "All right. Go on."

"Third, my house isn't always such a good place to be."

"How so?" I asked, remembering the depressing broken-down exterior.

"Well, it's plain old ugly for one thing."

"Oh, I wouldn't say that. . . ."

But Chris wouldn't tolerate any insincerity. "Come on, Dana. Talk straight with me."

"I guess it does look a little run-down," I confessed. "From the outside."

"Let's just say it's nothing like Jenny Baker's." Chris looked embarrassed.

I leaned my head on his shoulder. "Most people's houses aren't."

Chris shrugged. "Yeah, but . . ."

"Chris," I said, "anyone who cares about fancy houses and cars is really shallow, and you know I'm not like that."

"This is true." Chris smiled, as if he only then remembered he was talking to someone he'd known almost all his life. He rubbed his hands along the sun-warmed rock. "It's just that, well, the inside's pretty crummy too. My dad works really long shifts for the electric company. And when he's not working, he's sleeping. I try to keep the yard clean, but without his help, and with all the chores *inside* . . . And my stepmother, well, she's a strange story."

"What do you mean?" I asked.

"She's sort of depressed a lot of the time."

A clump of weeds poked their heads through a large crack in the rock. Chris snapped off a stalk and twirled it between his fingers. "And she drinks a lot, so . . . whatever."

"Do you . . . do you think much about your real mother?" I knew Chris's mother was dead, but I didn't know any of the circumstances.

Chris sighed. "I hardly knew her. I mean, I was only five."

"How did she die?" I asked gently.

A funny look passed over his face. "Cancer."

I swallowed my surprise with a thick gulp. I don't know what I expected him to tell me—maybe a car accident, or something less . . . familiar. I knew I should say something, but I felt overwhelmed with fear. There's nothing more traumatic than fighting cancer. But then to lose the battle—that's something I don't let myself think about. And every time I hear about someone who died from the disease, I shudder.

"I'm so—I'm so sorry," I said finally.

"It was a long time ago," Chris said, turning his attention to a bird calling in a tree overhead.

"Were you ever close to your stepmother? I mean, before she started drinking."

Chris shook his head. "The thing is, I'm pretty sure she's always been drinking. Secretly. Looking back on it, I don't think I've ever seen her sober." The bird soared from the tree. Chris and I watched him fly away.

95

We studied alcoholism in health class last year. The teacher spent a lot of time describing how painful it is to be the child of someone who drinks. I could imagine how upsetting it must be for Chris to live with his stepmother.

"What do you do about it?" I asked.

"There's really nothing I can do," he said. "I can only look out for myself. And I don't drink at all," he added.

"That's impressive."

He shrugged. "That's part of the reason I wanted to drive you home that night you were out with Aaron," he said, turning to look at me. "I get really uptight when people drink and drive. One beer is one too many, especially if you've got someone else's life in your car. That's how I got this mark in my eyebrow," he said, tracing the small, thin, hairless line that cut across his left eyebrow. "My stepmom got in an accident driving me home from school one day. I'll never forget it because it was my first day of eighth grade."

I gasped. "Chris, that's terrible!" I pictured Chris, young and vulnerable, his forehead bloody. I bit my lip.

"She was drunk. The cops gave her a Breathalyzer test and brought us down to the station. The gym teacher had to come get me at the hospital and drive me home."

"Where was your dad?"

"Working a double shift, then bailing his wife out of jail."

"Was she hurt?"

"Not seriously. Not seriously enough—I mean, not enough to get her to stop drinking." Chris frowned. "But I'll never forget it."

"Do you mind talking about this?" I asked him, resting my hand on his leg.

"Not really. I mean, I can't pretend anymore that it isn't there. Like I used to."

"What do you mean?"

He put his hand on top of mine. "Well, when I was little I used to lie to my friends about it. Like, I'd tell them my stepmom had a stomach flu to explain why she was in the bathroom all morning. Or I'd tell people she worked nights to explain why she slept so late. Stuff like that." He glanced at me with a worried expression, as if he wondered whether I thought that was a horrible thing to do.

"And people believed you?" I asked.

"Yeah, mostly they did. Except for Brian. He knew something was wrong with her. He just wouldn't let me lie to him about it."

"Did you tell him the truth?"

"Eventually I did. He must have told you," Chris said.

"He didn't." Brian had never told me any of this, and I felt strangely proud of him. I guess good friends don't betray each other's confidences—even to their sisters.

"Well, I'm sure he told your parents. That has to be why they let me come over for dinner almost every day." Chris paused for a moment, warming his face in the sun, shielding his eyes with his hand. "Your parents are the best, the way they let me hang out so much, and feed me," he said. "I don't know what I'd do if I couldn't spend time at your house."

"They are the best," I agreed. Hearing Chris say something so nice about my parents made me feel lucky. I don't know what I'd do if Mom were like Chris's stepmother—drunk, distracted, unavailable. It would be awful.

I felt sorry for Chris. I'd never had any idea he had to deal with so much stuff at home. Or that he was so strong. Or that with each passing hour, I would grow more and more in love with him.

"Close your eyes and count to ten," Chris said suddenly.

I obeyed. "Okay. One . . ."

I heard him stand up and scurry around.

"Two. You're not going to dump water on my head, right?"

"Promise."

"Three. So, what are you doing?"

"Getting something ready."

"Four. A campfire?"

"That would be dangerous."

I heard crumpling noises, then a crackling sound, like he was breaking twigs.

"Five. Are you building a stick castle?"

"What's a stick castle?"

"A sand castle but with sticks. Six."

"Nice try, but no. And don't peek." He threw his sweatshirt over my head. It smelled faintly like Clorox.

"Seven. You're making a bracelet out of tree bark."

"Getting warmer. Very warm."

"You're making a tanning salon out of tree bark. Eight."

He laughed. "Not that kind of warm."

"Nine. I'm fresh out of guesses, so I have to say . . . ten."

I tossed the sweatshirt off my head, opened my eyes, and squinted in the white-hot sunlight. Then I caught sight of Chris's surprise. He held it in the palm of his hand—a chunky silver ID bracelet on top of a crinkled paper bag. It glistened in the sunlight.

"I want you to have this," he said, reaching for my hand. "My mother gave it to me. She had it inscribed before she died."

I studied the bracelet. Two tiny engraved hearts decorated the front. He flipped the bracelet over so that I could read the inscription on the back.

"Christopher Mitchell Geller. My love will never die."

"She knew she was dying," he explained, fastening the chain around my wrist. "Her cancer was inoperable. She ordered this in a man's size because, well . . ." His face crumpled. ". . . because she knew she'd never live to see me become one."

He stared into my eyes. "I've carried this in my pocket since the funeral. Time for it to get some use."

I was overwhelmed with emotion. "I can't take this," I said. I held my arm out in front of me. The smooth, flat links sparkled as if they were wet. I loved Chris, and I wanted us to be close. But taking this gift from him felt wrong—as if I were intruding, venturing into a private place where I didn't belong. I began to undo the clasp.

He grabbed my hand to stop me. "Please. Just wear it for now, okay?"

"I can't, Chris." I took it off and held it in my palm.

"It will make me happy, really. I hardly ever talk about my mom. But I wanted you to know about her."

"I'm glad you told me," I said honestly.

He looked at me and hesitated, as if he were about to say something else and changed his mind.

"There's more?" I encouraged.

Chris nodded and took a deep breath.

"Tell me. Please?" I reached out with my empty hand and squeezed his fingers.

"You know I—I think I—"

He stopped and pursed his lips.

"What?" I asked, hoping he would say what I was feeling, what I wanted so badly to say back to him. Was it possible for us to have fallen in love so quickly?

"Never mind," Chris said. "You'll keep the bracelet, won't you?"

Everything between us was happening so fast, it scared me a little. But at the same time, everything felt right. So I kissed him and held out my wrist for him to refasten the bracelet.

I knew.

He loved me.

★　　★　　★

"Where have you been all day?" Brian asked as I jogged into the house at four o'clock. Chris had dropped me off a few blocks away so that no one would see us together. I eased into the house, hoping no one was there.

"Running," I lied, not looking at him. My face turned crimson. I don't like lying.

I plopped down on the tile floor in the kitchen and stretched. The ID bracelet jingled down my arm. I checked to make sure the inscription wasn't facing out. Nope—just the hearts. It was a friendship bracelet, I decided. From Kim. If anyone asked.

"Must've been an amazing run," Brian said, staring at me. "You're as red as the living room rug. And what's with that goofy smile?"

I twisted my mouth to get the grin of glee off my face.

"Endorphins." Runners' high was as good an excuse as I could muster on the spot.

"Kim called," he went on, pouring himself a bowl of cereal, his favorite afternoon snack.

"What did she say?"

"She said she's mad you haven't called back. She left a message last night."

"I'll go call her now," I decided, standing up.

"You know, Kim's pretty cool," Brian commented, digging a spoon into his bowl of cereal. "We talked for a while."

"She's the best," I agreed.

"She's pretty too," Brian added, picking up the

cereal box to read it, as if it might tell him something fascinating.

"Gorgeous," I confirmed.

"I can't believe she gets up every morning at five-thirty to stretch out for dance class," he said, still staring at the cereal box. "I mean, what a commitment. Did you know she pays for her own dance classes?"

"Incredible, isn't it?" I said. What was the deal with him? He'd known Kim for years, but he was talking as if he'd just met her! "I'll go call her now."

I couldn't wait to tell Kim what had happened with Chris. And I wondered if Kim would have as many good things to say about Brian as he had to say about her!

"Did you see Chris today?" Brian asked as I headed for the door. "I called him a bunch of times but he wasn't around."

Brian's question caught me completely off guard. I weighed my options in a split second. "Yeah, he saw me jogging, so we ran together for a while," would sound perfectly normal. I mean, Chris and I were both on the track team—we ran together a lot. But what if my face revealed the truth?

I had never flat-out lied to my brother before that day. Before Chris.

"Chris?" I said, turning to face Brian. "Nope. Haven't seen him." I turned and walked away.

Later that night, my parents and Brian and I

hung out for a while watching TV. I hadn't talked to Brian much since I got home—I was still afraid I'd slip up and admit that I'd spent the day with Chris.

When the phone rang, I jumped off the sofa to get it. *It's probably Kim returning my call from before,* I thought, glad for the distraction.

"Hello?"

"I was hoping you'd pick up the phone."

"Hey," I said, trying to keep my voice calm.

"Who is it?" my dad asked, muting the TV.

It was Chris. "It's for me," I told him. "I'll take it upstairs." I dashed up to my room, hollered, "I got it," and waited to hear Dad hang up the extension.

I sat on my windowsill and cradled the phone beneath my ear. "Hi," I said excitedly.

"I miss you," Chris replied.

"I miss *you!*" I had done more than miss him. I had thought about him nonstop from the moment I got out of his car.

But I also felt guilty about lying to Brian, and I knew something had to be done soon. Before I could say anything, Chris spoke again.

"Quick—turn on the radio," he said. "99X."

"Hang on a sec." I turned my clock radio on. The dial was already set for 99X, the only alternative rock station in the city. The deejay was reading a commercial for Benton's bookstore.

"Why are you having me listen to commercials?" I asked.

"Shhh. Just wait."

So I waited, and I listened.

". . . Benton's, open until midnight Monday through Saturday, with fresh coffee all day long and half-price cakes and cookies after nine o'clock each night. Next up we have a special request for the new Scorching Stones single 'When I'm with You,' going out to Dana L. from a secret admirer. Hope you're listening, Dana—this one's for you."

"Oh, my gosh," I said to Chris.

"Shhh! Listen."

I knew the words by heart, but they took on a special meaning now, each line making me think about how I felt when I was with Chris.

> *When I'm with you,*
> *The world just disappears.*
> *'Cause I'm with you*
> *Everything I want is clear*
> *Since I found you*
> *I'm everywhere you are*
> *My dreams run strong and far*
> *When I'm with you. . . .*

"Chris, I can't believe you did this," I whispered. The song went on, each line more and more meaningful, describing our situation perfectly.

> *From my secret life inside*
> *They won't see us*

Our secret love is true
And all I want to do
Is be here with you.

"You know, I had a perfect day with you," Chris said when the song ended.

"Perfect," I echoed.

"It'll be weird seeing you in school tomorrow. You know, pretending you're still just my friend's sister."

I didn't want to pretend. I wanted to show the world how Chris and I felt about each other. But that would mean letting Brian know. It wasn't fair that I had to lie to him about something so important. Why did he have to make that stupid rule?

"I wish we didn't have to worry about pretending," I complained. "We have to tell Brian eventually."

"Not now. Just lay low," Chris said, his voice tense.

"You really think that's best?" I asked.

"I'm not sure," Chris admitted. "But I need to think about things for a while. I need to figure out how to tell him."

Fair enough, I thought. Chris must be as worried as I was. Much as I wanted to be truthful, there were so many things to consider. Every time I imagined having a heart-to-heart conversation with Brian, I felt completely overwhelmed. I couldn't imagine how to explain things to him.

It's only for a little while, I told myself. *How much can a few days matter?*

"I should probably hang up," Chris said. He laughed nervously. "I have to call Brian."

"Okay," I replied quietly. I wanted to say more, to tell Chris again how much this weekend had meant to me. How much *he* meant to me. But I couldn't seem to get the words out.

"See you tomorrow," he said.

"Chris?"

"Yeah?"

He *had* to know how strong my feelings were. I *had* to be brave.

"I'm really loving . . . this," I said, chickening out.

"Good," he replied. "Because I'm really loving you."

Nine

EARLY MONDAY MORNING, while I was yanking an old sweatshirt out of my locker, Chris tapped me on the back.

"Hey!" I reached out to hug him, then stopped myself.

"C'mere," Chris said. At the end of the hall there's a huge kiosk covered with posters—school play announcements and athletic tournaments and ads for specials at local stores. Chris and I ducked behind it and twisted our heads to see if the coast was clear. No teachers, no kids milling around, and most important, no Brian.

He kissed me like crazy.

"Let's skip track practice today," he suggested when we came up for air. "And we'll go for a drive."

"What's my excuse? Coach Franklin will have a fit!"

"Tell him you have to take a very important drive with a drop-dead gorgeous guy."

"Oh, good one," I laughed. "That'll work."

"No? Okay, then after track practice we'll hang out for a while, all right? Maybe take a short drive."

"Hey, guys!" Brian called.

I spun around to see him at the corner of the hallway about ten feet behind us.

I panicked. I could feel the blood rushing down to my feet and turning my body into a statue. Chris, in an effort to seem totally casual, gestured for Brian to come over. I automatically stepped away from Chris, separating myself from any signs of an embrace.

"What's up, Bri?" Chris said.

"What's up with you?" Brian answered, giving Chris one of those guy pseudohandshakes.

"Just lending Dana my—"

"Compass," I interrupted. I caught Chris's eye, and immediately I felt bad that I'd lied for both of us.

"Hey, Dana," Brian said. "I'll pick you up after track practice today."

Without thinking, I looked at Chris. Then I shook my head.

"Uh, well—"

"Mom told me to tell you to be home by six, so I'll meet you by the track at five-thirty."

"Whatever," I said, trying to disguise my disappointment.

"Anyway, I'm late for my SG meeting, so I'll catch you later." SG is student government. I had forgotten that Brian had meetings every Monday morning before first period. I'd have to learn to be more careful if Chris and I were going to continue this secret relationship.

"That sort of puts a damper on our driving plans," I murmured when Brian left.

"Tell me about it."

"I don't like lying to Brian." I lowered my voice in case one of Brian's friends was poking around nearby.

"I feel pretty lousy about it too, Dana."

"Brian has never lied to me."

"Me neither," Chris said sadly. "Brian's the best."

"So we *have* to be honest with him," I argued. "The sooner the better." My guilty conscience triggered an image of my fourth-grade classroom, the wall full of helpful slogans written on bold, bright sheets of construction paper: "Do unto others as you would have them do unto you." "Honesty is the best policy."

"I want to tell him, Dana. I really do," Chris said. He sounded a little desperate. "The first thing I thought of after you and I got together was, 'I can't wait to tell Brian about this awesome girl!' "

I smiled.

"But then I remembered that the awesome girl is his sister, and she's the one girl in school I'm supposed to stay away from. Do you have any idea how lousy that made me feel?"

"Of course! Don't you think I want my brother to know about this fantastic guy I'm seeing?"

"Ironic, huh," Chris said.

"It is."

It was more than ironic. Lying to Brian was already becoming a real burden. And something was missing without Brian in the picture—something important. I realized I felt more than guilt. I wanted Brian to be a part of everything significant in my life.

The bell rang, piercing and intrusive. "I have to go," Chris said abruptly. No real chance for a kiss good-bye. Not after such a close call.

"Bye," I said sadly.

Kim caught me pacing back and forth in front of her locker after first period.

"I couldn't call you back last night," she explained. She was still in her dance clothes, parachute pants hoisted up to her rib cage. "My mom was on the phone, and—"

"I have to talk to you," I interrupted, pulling her close to me. The smell of resin and baby powder wafted around her.

"Is it bad?"

"It's incredible."

"Is it Chris?"

I nodded furiously.

"Is it about Saturday night, the concert? He asked you out?"

"That's the least of it."

Kim's big eyes widened in amazement. "I knew it! Didn't I tell you something would happen?"

The bell rang for second period, its shrill sound echoing off the walls.

"What's the most of it?" she asked eagerly.

I leaned forward so that no one could overhear me. "I think I'm falling in love."

"Give me two hours," Chris said after track practice on Thursday, "and it will be the best night of your life."

"Pretty sure of yourself, huh?" I teased, wiping my neck with his hand towel. I pressed it to my face and inhaled his earthy smell. The days had flown by, the week punctuated by secret encounters with Chris, and by my counting the minutes until we could be together during track practice. Every time I ran by him, my insides fluttered and my face got hot. I loved the way he looked at me.

Then, inevitably, I'd think of Brian—and guilt replaced excitement in a flash. The longer this secrecy went on, the angrier Brian would be when he found out. But I just didn't know what to do.

"At the moment, I'm totally sure of myself," Chris said, lifting a bottle of water to his lips. "I happen to know your parents are going out tonight and left you and Brian money to order a pizza."

"You've been spying at my house?"

"Brian told me. Tell him you're going to study somewhere, and then you and I can go get some dinner. Do you realize we've never eaten a meal alone together in a public place?"

"Too risky," I said, taking his water. In the park

or at the waterfall we were safe, but restaurants were obviously out of the question.

"Not tonight—none of our friends go out to dinner on a Thursday. So call Brian, tell him you're going to the library or something—"

"Then I have to call Kim so that she'll cover for me."

"She knows about us?" Chris asked nervously.

"Well, she *is* my best friend." I couldn't imagine not telling Kim.

Chris looked stricken. Suddenly I realized what I'd just said. I mean, Brian was *his* best friend—and the one person he couldn't tell about us.

"You know," Chris said, "I want to tell everyone I know about you and me. I want most of all to tell *Brian* about you and me."

"So let's tell him," I said. Plain and simple.

"Not yet." Chris took back his water and poured it over my head. It felt refreshing after a tough workout. "Hit the showers," he said with the same authoritative voice as our coach. "I'll meet you in the parking lot."

I dashed across the field to the girls' locker room, took a cool shower, and called Kim from the pay phone inside. She answered on the first ring.

"All you know," I said, "is that I went over to Jenny Baker's house tonight to study."

"When in reality?"

"I'm going out with Chris."

"And your family?"

"My parents are out. They left us pizza money, so Brian's all alone."

"I could go keep him company," she suggested.

"You'd do that for me?" I asked skeptically. It would be great knowing Brian was trapped at my house.

"My pleasure," Kim replied.

"Well, thanks. Just don't say anything that will make me look obvious," I warned her.

"Please," she answered, as if I should know better. "You know I'm trustworthy."

Yeah, but I'm not, I thought miserably. I hung up with Kim and dashed toward the parking lot, drying my hair with my fingers. Chris had the car running, as if we had to make a quick getaway. As soon as I fastened my seat belt, we took off.

"You never know who's watching," he said, turning on the radio. "So where to?"

I shrugged.

"I know Mexican food's your favorite."

"How do you know?" I asked.

"Because the night before all your big tests, your mom makes burritos for dinner." He glanced at me for a nod of approval. "So Mexican it is." I was impressed he'd paid such close attention to my life. I wondered what other details he'd noticed about me. Five minutes later, we pulled into the Border Café.

It felt as if we were playing hooky, going out on a date on a weeknight. I liked it. Over a huge plate of nachos with everything, Chris listed all the ways he'd figured out we could spend time together without getting caught. He had a dozen schemes and plots and ways to cover our tracks. It was exciting to make so many secret plans. But at the same time, I couldn't shake the feeling that we were doing something wrong.

"What happens if Brian finds out about us before we tell him?" I asked.

Chris scooped up the last bit of guacamole on a chip and handed it to me.

"He can't find out," he said firmly.

"Chris," I argued, "we're an accident waiting to happen. I can't believe we haven't gotten caught already."

Chris frowned. "What do you mean?"

"Well, think about it," I said. "The change in the way we treat each other is so obvious. How long can Brian go on missing it? And what about all those times we've met behind the school, or in empty classrooms? Someone, at some point, is going to see us. And then Brian will find out for sure."

"I suppose that's true," Chris conceded, biting into a chip.

"So let's make a plan," I said firmly.

"Like what? Should I stop by and say, 'Hey Bri, me and Dana are a couple now. Want to watch a video?'"

I giggled. "Not exactly."

"Seriously, Dana. I want to tell Brian. But what do we say? How do we start?"

"How about we go out for some food," I said slowly. "Somewhere neutral. Then we tell him we have some really good news for him, but we're a little uncomfortable about the whole thing. And most of all, we want to make sure he's happy about it too."

Chris looked interested but nervous. I didn't feel nervous, though. The idea was so simple and straightforward. How could it fail?

"Go on," he prompted.

"Then I can tell him how I've known you for a long time and totally trust you—he'll understand that because he feels the same way—and that you and I got to know each other really well, and then—"

"Don't give him the 'one thing led to another' speech," Chris said, rolling his eyes.

"But that's what really happened."

"But it sounds lame. I'll tell him I got to know you as a person, as someone more than his kid sister. And that I think you're pretty terrific. He'll agree with that part, at least," Chris said excitedly, following my lead.

"Right." Relief rushed through me.

"He'll ask how long we've been together," Chris continued.

"We'll say a short time. He doesn't have to know every intimate detail." I finished my Coke. "Keeping some things to ourselves isn't the same as lying."

"He'll want to know why we kept it a secret," Chris warned.

"We'll tell him we needed some time to figure things out."

"Which is the truth," he agreed.

"If you think about it," I said, "we're being totally upstanding about the whole thing—how we got together, our feelings for each other, how we want to tell the truth about it. . . ."

"Our respect for Brian's opinion," Chris added.

"Exactly." I paused for a moment. It all sounded so easy, but at the same time I wondered if everything really would go according to plan. I couldn't guarantee that the script would play itself out the way Chris and I had conceived it.

"Actually," Chris said, breaking my train of thought, "we haven't done anything really wrong. You can't help the way you feel about somebody."

"But you can help lying," I said.

"Right. So we're not going to lie anymore." Chris folded his arms across his chest. "Case closed."

It felt good to be doing the right thing. Just reaching a decision calmed my nervous stomach. Suddenly, I wanted more nachos. I smeared my index finger on the plate to scoop up crumbs.

"And maybe when he sees how great things are—" Chris went on.

"Maybe—" I said, hopefully. I crossed my greasy fingers for luck and Chris kissed them.

"So when should we do it?" he asked.

"Tomorrow?" I suggested. I wanted to get it over with.

"Maybe Friday night's a bad idea," Chris said. "Brian always wants to go home and sleep on

Fridays—you know he gets into a bad mood whenever he can't nap."

"Good point."

"This weekend is impossible because of that senior camping trip," Chris went on. "We leave at five on Saturday morning and won't be home until late Monday night."

"You wouldn't tell him without me, right?"

"I hate the thought of keeping this from him for the whole senior trip . . . but no, I won't tell him," Chris promised. "You should be there too."

"So how about Monday night?"

"I think weeknights are a bad idea in general," Chris said. "Especially with finals right around the corner."

"True. Homework, stress, potential awkwardness in school the next day."

"We'll tell him next Saturday," Chris said resolutely. "The three of us can spend the day together and that way Brian won't feel left out."

"Excellent."

As Chris relaxed in the high-backed wicker chair, I could tell that he felt as good about our decision as I did. Brian might flip out about things at first, but I had faith he'd calm down and accept my relationship with Chris. Maybe he'd even be happy about it.

On Friday night, my ability to lie was put to the ultimate test.

Mom was cooking spaghetti and meatballs for

supper. I could smell the garlic before Brian and I came in the door.

"Yum!" he called, dropping his knapsack on the stairs. Exhaustion made his footsteps heavy and deliberate.

"Put your stuff away, Brian," my mother called from the kitchen. She couldn't see him, but she knew he always left a mess in the entrance hall.

"Smells great, Mom," I said, hustling toward the stove to taste the sauce. My mom presented me with a steaming spoonful.

"Careful," she said, cupping her hand below the spoon. "It's hot."

I slurped in a small taste, the perfect combination of sweetness and salt. "Hot, but good. When's dinner?"

"Soon. Honey, would you set the table?" she asked, gesturing toward the cabinets. "Dad's hung up in a Board of Ed meeting, so it's just the three of us." She paused, then added, "Unless Chris wants to come by for dinner. There's plenty, and he hasn't been here all week."

The sound of his name made me unexpectedly nervous. And suddenly, the thought of getting through a meal with him in my own kitchen seemed impossible.

A week from tomorrow and the truth will be out in the open, I thought. *Hang in there.*

"I think Chris has plans," I mumbled. I focused on the task at hand, removing three pasta bowls from the cupboard. "He mentioned something about it."

118

"I already invited him," Brian said, coming into the kitchen and throwing his jacket on a chair. "I'll call and see if he's coming."

"You can call from your room," my mom replied, handing him back his jacket. "And while you're at it, hang this up in your closet."

I moved with slow steps to the table. I didn't know whether to look forward to seeing Chris, or to dread him coming.

"What's wrong?" Mom asked, removing condiments from the refrigerator and handing them to me. Parmesan cheese. Butter.

I can't lie to my mother. She sees right through me.

"Later, okay?" I pleaded.

"Okay." Out came the salad dressing. Bacon bits. Milk. I carefully arranged the table, my hands trembling with anxiety. I was dying to spend tonight with Chris, especially since he was going to be away until Monday. But not here . . . not now . . . not in front of everyone. . . .

Brian trotted down the stairs. I kept my eyes fixed on the napkins, which I had folded and re-folded and set perfectly alongside each bowl.

"There's no answer. He must be on his way," Brian said.

"Terrific," Mom said. "Dana, could you come and help me upstairs for a second?"

"Come and help me upstairs" was the family code for "let's talk privately for a minute." Brian knew that, but he was too busy eating a meatball with his fingers to care.

119

"So what's wrong?" my mother said quietly when we were in her bedroom, safely out of earshot.

"Nothing's really wrong," I explained. My mother's apron showed faded stains from a lifetime of family feasts—homemade chocolate cake, holiday dinners, and pancake breakfasts. I thought of Chris's stepmother, and the fact that she'd probably never made a meal for him. He wouldn't want my pity, but I couldn't help it. I felt sorry for him.

"Well, something's on your mind," Mom said, smoothing the worry lines on my forehead.

"I think it's really great that we have Chris here for dinner so much," I said brightly. "I know he really appreciates it."

"I'm sure he does." My mother narrowed her piercing blue eyes at me.

"Because I think his stepmother is sort of . . . preoccupied," I went on.

"I think the Gellers have a pretty rough time of it," she admitted. "Money's tight, and, of course, a death in the family makes things nearly impossible to repair." I knew Mom knew more than she was letting on, but she was protecting Chris's privacy as much as I was.

"He's such a good friend to Brian," I said, suddenly overwhelmed with guilt. I stared at my lap.

"What are you getting at?" my mother urged.

I couldn't speak.

"You and Chris have feelings for each other."

It was a statement, not a question. I looked up at her, embarrassed, but relieved.

"Major feelings. Definite feelings."

A smile spread across her face. "I think that's wonderful," she said.

"But it's all so sudden, Mom. I haven't had any time to think."

"Sometimes, you don't need to think," she said, putting her arm around me.

"Is that how it happened with you and Dad?" I asked, trying to picture my parents before they got married. Did they kiss by waterfalls, exchange secrets? Did they have a special song and did Dad give Mom sentimental jewelry? Did she fall for him in a single weekend? Was falling in love with Dad the best and scariest thing in her life?

"Well, I was much more shy than you are," Mom said.

I couldn't picture my self-confident mother ever feeling shy.

"But that's not the point," she continued. "I know Chris is a special young man, as corny as that sounds. And I know there isn't a better girl on this earth—"

"Mom, cut it out."

"Than you. So if you have feelings for each other, I think that's great."

The doorbell rang. I heard Brian usher Chris inside. "Hey, Ma," he yelled. "Something's burning!"

Suddenly I could smell the garlic bread beginning to scorch. My mother and I headed downstairs to save it.

I tugged on her arm to stop her for a moment. "Brian doesn't know," I whispered.

"Why not?" she asked, surprised.

"I told you how after that whole episode with Aaron, he made a big deal about how I wasn't allowed to date his friends," I explained. "But Chris and I are going to tell him the truth. Soon."

My mother was rarely judgmental, but this time she made her opinion clear.

"Good. Because Brian will be more upset that you're lying to him than about the fact that his sister is dating his best friend."

"I don't know about that," I said. But she was right about one thing. Brian didn't deserve to be lied to.

"Wow—this looks really great, Mrs. Lipton," I heard Chris call out.

"Have a seat, guys," my mom replied, walking into the kitchen. I followed her nervously.

"Hey, Dana," Chris said, as if nothing had changed between us.

"Hey." My throat tightened. I felt totally self-conscious.

"Hot garlic bread," my mother said, proudly displaying the crusty, slightly scorched loaf. Brian tore off a huge chunk.

The meal lasted longer than my appetite. Everyone else seemed to be fine, but the tension within me was heavier than Mom's meatballs. Chris never even shot a knowing look my way. Nothing. How could he stand it? He ate three helpings, chatted with Brian about sports, thanked my mom profusely, and offered to do the dishes before he left. I, on the other hand, sat paralyzed, force-fed myself each bite, and couldn't take my eyes off Chris's every move.

Finally, he caught my eye. A rush of excitement exploded in my chest.

Chris turned to Brian. "You mind lending me your duffel bag for the class trip?"

"It's upstairs," Brian replied, pushing his chair away from the table. "I'll get it."

My mother, no doubt sensing the tension in the air, turned her back to us and began loading the dishwasher. We had ten seconds to be almost alone.

"Are you psyched to go camping?" I asked. I missed Chris already.

"Sure am," he said, shaking his head "no" behind my mother's back.

Then he slipped me a note. I began to open it, but he frowned.

"Not now," he mouthed. Brian returned and threw Chris his blue duffel.

"Thanks," Chris said, catching it. "I'll see you at the school tomorrow."

Brian groaned. "Yeah, at five A.M."

Chris grinned. "Good night, Liptons. Thanks for another fantastic meal."

"You're always welcome—you know that," Mom said. She winked at me and I smiled a thank-you her way. Then she said, "Brian, it's your turn to do the dishes."

"Yup," he answered grudgingly, taking the soiled sponge.

The instant Chris had gone and Brian's back was to me, I unfolded the note.

Our secret love is true, and all I want to
do is be here with you.

Guilt and excitement are a terrible combination.
The more ecstatic I felt, the guiltier I felt. Brian had
no clue what was going on—I was sure of it. I was
equally sure that lying to him was the wrong
choice.

I couldn't wait to come clean. Eight more days.

Ten

CHRIS SHOWED UP for track practice an hour late on Tuesday. I was on my sixteenth lap and fading fast when he caught up to me.

"Where were you?" I asked. "Franklin was peeved." Our coach demanded total commitment from the team. When someone's dedication diminished, he or she got cut.

"I had something to do," he said. We were running at the same pace, but I was out of breath.

"It's no fun when you're not here," I said, the words chopped off as I gasped for oxygen.

"Geller!" Coach Franklin yelled in the megaphone. "Quit your flirting and concentrate on running." I laughed, the giggles spitting out in short, puffing spurts.

"Got to get moving," he said apologetically.

I tried my best to run faster.

"Wait," I said. "I'll keep up."

We synchronized our stride. "You didn't tell Brian anything, did you?" I huffed.

"I thought we agreed to tell him together?"

"I know, but I thought that maybe over the weekend . . ."

"I considered it," he admitted. "But then I didn't know what to tell him."

"The truth?" I suggested.

"You make it sound so easy."

"Do you still think we should tell him together?" I asked.

"I don't know. He might feel like we're ganging up on him," Chris said. "But don't worry. We'll figure something out."

"This is your last warning, Geller. Ten laps in ten minutes or you're out of next week's meet. Quit distracting him, Lipton!"

Chris took off like a rocket, zooming around the loop as fast as he could.

My foot cramped, so I slowed to a brisk walk for the last half mile. Chris blew tiny, barely visible kisses my way with each pass.

The team scattered at five-thirty, but Chris had four laps to go. I waited on the bleachers and watched him while he ran. His powerful legs glided effortlessly over the track. Sprinting came as easily to him as walking or brushing his teeth. His dark hair blew straight up in the sticky air, and he wiped his face with the tail of his shirt.

He waved at me and I waved back. I realized

126

again how much I liked the way he looked—solid, natural, and strong.

The late-day sun cast a shadow on the track. That's when Chris stopped running and sat on the dusty path with his head in his knees.

"You all right?" I yelled, running down to him.

"Fine. Just a little dizzy."

I leaned over and patted his back. "You need some water?"

"No, I'm fine," he said, lifting his head. He looked up at me in amazement. "You look incredibly beautiful."

"You're dangerously ill," I teased, sitting next to him.

"Sick with love," he said, flashing me a goofy grin.

"Seriously, what happened to you?"

"I gave blood today," he explained, letting out a deep breath. "That's why I was late."

"Is everything okay?"

"Fine." He paused. "I did something I think you might like," he said.

"Tell me."

"I gave a blood sample to the Bone Marrow Donors Registry," he answered.

I was stunned. "You what?"

"I signed up to be a donor. In case, well, in case someone needs bone marrow. Like you did. I must be a match for somebody somewhere, right?"

I was speechless. My eyes filled with tears.

"I figured," he continued, wiping a tear off my cheek, "some random person in some unknown place was thoughtful enough to donate the bone marrow that saved your life. So why shouldn't I do the same thing?"

After my transplant, my parents had joined the donors registry program, but that seemed like the sort of thing parents of sick kids would do automatically. I knew that someday I'd ask my husband to do the same, but I never expected one of my friends—even my boyfriend—to do it on their own.

Tears flowed freely down my face.

"Who knows," Chris said, watching me affectionately. "Maybe some eight-year-old girl with leukemia will need a bone marrow transplant so she can grow up and have an incredibly perfect high-school senior fall in love with her."

I took Chris in my arms. I tried to thank him, to let him know how grateful I was, but the words wouldn't come out. I kissed him.

"You don't have to say anything, Dana," he said quietly. "I know."

Chris had told me to save Friday night for him—our last night before Brian would learn the truth. So when Brian asked Kim and me if we wanted to go to the movies, I told him I was too tired. Ironic, since being too tired is usually Brian's excuse for not going out on a Friday night. I think he's actually just lazy.

"You sure?" he pressed, urging me to change my mind. "It's a sneak preview of the new Schwarzenegger movie."

"Who's going with you?" I asked, trying to look exhausted. I lay sprawled on the couch, a blanket draped over me.

"A bunch of people. You guys should come."

Kim sat on the easy chair, her back straight, channel surfing.

"I'll go," she said, looking at me to see if I'd have a change of heart.

"Great," Brian said enthusiastically. "Dana?"

"I think I'll stay in tonight, thanks," I said, wondering what Chris's excuse was to get out of going to the movie with Brian.

"Come on, Dana," Kim said eagerly. "Come with us."

I shot her a look that said, "Cut it out, I have other plans." She got it.

"Well," she said, "I guess if you're that tired, you should crash."

"Absolutely," I agreed, flashing her a small smile while Brian scanned the room as if he'd misplaced something.

"Your loss," Brian said. "Tell Mom and Dad I'll be home around midnight, okay?"

"Okay, if I'm still awake when they get home." I made a mental note: Brian would be back by midnight; my parents said they'd be home by eleven. I'd have at least three hours of uninterrupted Chris time.

Brian dug his hand between the cushions under me. "Have you seen my wallet?"

"I think it's upstairs in the bathroom," I said. "Why don't you check there?"

Brian darted upstairs. Kim bolted from the easy chair and sat on the arm of the couch.

"You're seeing Chris?" she asked.

"At eight."

"Tell me where you guys are going," she asked, "so that I can make sure Brian doesn't wind up there."

"Not sure. Probably Napoli's pizza." Napoli's was outside the heart of the city, fifteen miles from the Cineplex. We'd never get caught there. "I hope you don't mind spending another night baby-sitting Brian," I joked.

Kim shook her head. "I had fun hanging out with him last time."

I heard Brian stomp downstairs.

"We should go," he said, checking his watch. "I'm sure the line is huge."

"I'm set," Kim said, standing up and tossing her hair over her shoulder. "I'll call you tomorrow, Dana."

"Definitely."

As soon as I heard them leave I grabbed the phone to call Chris, but a car pulled into the driveway before I finished dialing. Brian must have forgotten something. I hung up and went to the door to let him in.

But it was Chris.

"What are you doing here?" I said, delighted. "I was just about to call you."

"I knew Brian was going to the movies tonight, so I figured the coast was clear."

"Barely," I said. "You just missed him."

"I guess fate is in our favor," he replied, kissing me.

"Mmm." A pang of guilt lodged in my chest. But that was quickly replaced with the joy I felt being with Chris. "How'd you get out of going with him?"

"I have a raging fever," he said, "and a horrible sore throat." He coughed.

"You poor thing," I teased.

"I—I'm so wiped out, I have to sit down right here, right now. . . ." He plunked down on the top step, pulling me with him. ". . . and kiss you."

Perfect, I thought. The nearby streetlamp illuminated our driveway, casting a soft, grainy, black-and-white movie glow all around us. *We're all alone.*

"Where are your parents?" Chris asked suddenly.

"At a dinner party."

"We're all by ourselves here?"

"For a while."

The news seemed to cheer Chris up. He kissed me as if we hadn't seen each other for months.

"I love this," he said, kissing my chin. "I love kissing you."

"Me too," I said, recalling for a moment how I used to practice kissing my pillow. I could never imagine how fantastic it would feel to be kissed back. My arms quivered and my face felt hot. *I could do this all night,* I thought.

"So tomorrow we tell Brian?" I asked, my lips brushing his.

131

"Definitely." He pulled me closer.

My entire body felt absorbed by Chris. I wanted to learn every inch of him by heart. I kissed the chicken-pox scar below his ear. His arms felt strong and familiar around my waist. His hair curled at the edges in the humidity, and I stroked the smooth, feathery ends.

Cars drove by, but I barely heard them, their horns and stereos fading into the distance. My neighbor's dog howled incessantly, which made us laugh between kisses. A car rumbled to a stop nearby and a door slammed, but I didn't care.

Hurried footsteps. The faint jingling of keys. Nothing could distract my attention from loving Chris.

"I see you've made a miraculous recovery," Brian's voice said.

Brian!

Instinctively, I yanked myself out of Chris's embrace, but it was too late. I was in the midst of the moment I had feared every day, the incident I prayed would never actually take place. Brian's lips were pursed so tight they seemed to have disappeared. His entire face flushed with anger.

It took a moment for everything to sink in. Then it hit me like hot lead pouring down on my head. This was a total disaster.

I wanted to die.

Chris bolted to his feet.

"I thought you were going to the movies!" I blurted out stupidly.

"Sold out. Guess you didn't plan for that to happen."

"Uh, listen, Bri," Chris said. "Dana and I were just, uh—"

"I'm not an idiot. I have eyes," Brian snapped. "Did you want to make a jerk out of me? Or is it just that you didn't care?"

He pushed past Chris and stalked up the steps to the front door. Then he turned to me. I still sat helplessly on the front steps, pleading with my eyes for Brian to calm down.

"So, Dana," Brian said, "how long have you been lying to me?"

"I wanted to tell you for a while now, but—"

"A while now? Oh, that's great," Brian shouted. "That's just great." He shook his head in disbelief. "You know, Chris, you were there the night that whole thing happened with Dana and Aaron."

"Things were different then. I—" Chris began. "I—"

"You were there when I decided my friends were off-limits to Dana. Were you two seeing each other then?"

"Of course we weren't!" I cried.

"Well, it doesn't matter now," he said, turning his back on us. "Do whatever you want, Chris. You're not my friend anymore. Date my sister or whatever else you want. But don't talk to me, got it? Just don't talk to me."

Brian slammed the door so hard the front windows rattled.

Chris and I stared at each other.

Was this really the end of their friendship? Had we betrayed Brian's trust forever?

I hate myself, I thought.

"What happens now?" I choked out.

Chris didn't answer. He continued to look at me for a moment. Then he ran to his car and took off.

Eleven

BRIAN AND CHRIS might have needed some cooling-down time, but I couldn't stand to leave things this way.

Maybe I can persuade Brian that Chris and I are meant to be together, I thought. *Maybe if I just talk calmly and tell him how good Chris has been to me, he'll be happy for us.*

I went into the den where Brian sat in front of the TV. He didn't even acknowledge my presence.

"What are you watching?" I asked.

"Television," he said.

"Oh, I see." I felt like an idiot. After a few strained minutes of Brian ignoring me, I asked, "So, no movie, huh?"

"Obviously."

"What did you end up doing?"

"Nothing as interesting as what you were doing."

Score one for Brian. I forged ahead. "What happened to Kim?"

"I drove her home. What should I have done, made a pass at her?"

Score two. I was losing fast.

"Can we please just talk about this whole thing for a minute?" I begged.

"What is there to say? You're with Chris. Chris is with you. I'm totally lame for not catching on—I bet that concert you went to was a date—and my sister and best friend are total liars. End of discussion." He still wouldn't look at me, his eyes fixed on the rapidly changing TV stations.

I sat on the other side of the couch so that he'd have to look past me to see the TV. "That's not all there is to say, Brian. Just hear me out." He said nothing, so I continued. "Chris and I have a really special relationship. Neither of us planned it, but it all just fell into place, totally naturally. We've grown closer every day."

"That's what all the girls say about Chris," Brian scoffed. His words pierced through me like a sliver of ice.

"What do you mean?" I asked, wishing he would look at me.

"You know, he treats them real nice, makes them feel special, and then he just changes his mind and moves on to the next one." Brian spoke as if he knew the speech by heart.

"This is different," I assured him. *Isn't it?* I thought, a pang of fear shivering down my spine.

"That's what Joanna Winterson said," Brian told me.

"She just loves to gossip," I answered lamely.

Suddenly, Brian did look at me. His eyes were full of pain. "Why do you think I told you my friends were off-limits? Do you think I'm some kind of villain, out to make your life miserable? Or that I have some moral problem with your having a boyfriend? Do you think it's my personal mission to keep you single?"

"No." The truth is, I had never thought that. But I also never thought I needed as much protection as Brian seemed to think I did. Then again, I wasn't exactly experienced at dating and boys. Maybe Brian really did know better.

Brian kept talking. "I don't want you dating my friends because it's a guaranteed way for you to get hurt. Chris is no exception, Dana. He's a great friend, or at least he was once. He's good to the guys. But dating him is a definite way for you to end up miserable."

I didn't believe him. I couldn't.

"He's never been faithful to a girl. There's a long list of Chris's exes comparing notes on his routine."

I'd heard those girls comparing notes, like Brian said. But the Chris they complained about—the one who didn't call and stood them up and moved on to new girlfriends without a good-bye or an apology—that wasn't the Chris I knew. The Chris I knew gave me the bracelet his dying mother had given him. The Chris I knew had signed up for the donors registry program. The Chris I knew loved me thoroughly, completely.

"But do whatever you want, Dana," Brian finished. "You're a big girl. You'll get hurt, but you'll survive."

He was right. I had survived leukemia. I could certainly survive losing Chris. If my brother and I never got along again, I could survive that too. Couldn't I? But I wouldn't be happy about living through either of those things. How had I gotten myself into such a horrible situation? I couldn't bear the thought of losing Chris *or* Brian.

Brian's attention shifted back to the TV. I stood up, dizzy and disoriented. I felt as if a tornado had just swept me up and dropped me in another part of the world. What would possibly make Chris treat *me* differently than he did everyone else? Could I have fooled myself for these past few weeks? Nobody knew Chris better than Brian. If he truly believed Chris would hurt me, maybe he knew what he was talking about.

"I just wish you hadn't lied to me," Brian said quietly. "Both of you. I didn't deserve to be lied to."

I turned around.

"We didn't want to lie to you," I said, my voice quivering. "You didn't give us any choice. But we didn't *want* to lie."

"You did, though. Every single day."

That was the final blow. Brian was right. There was no excuse for lying, period. Especially to someone as honest and decent as Brian, someone who trusted me and looked out for me and had always been a great friend to Chris. I was ashamed of myself, and there was nothing I could do or say to make things better.

Later that night, I called Kim.

"What happened?" she asked immediately. "Did Brian ask where you were? I tried to convince him to see another movie or something, but he wanted to go home."

"I know," I whispered.

"Was he mad that you went out anyway?" she asked. Then she gasped. "Chris didn't walk you to the door after you got home from Napoli's, did he?"

I had completely forgotten about my plan to take Chris to Napoli's. Now I wished we had just hopped in the car and gone there, first thing. Then we would have told Brian the truth tomorrow, and nobody would have gotten hurt.

"We never got to Napoli's," I told Kim, the tears thick in my throat. "We were making out on the front steps, and then Brian—"

"Oh no," she cried. "I knew Brian would think it was weird you went out, but I just figured you and Chris would already be gone by the time he got home."

"No."

"Yikes! Dana, what did he say?"

"Well, he's more angry than I've ever seen him." I sniffled.

"That will pass," she said, trying her best to reassure me. "He'll realize how happy you are with Chris and the whole thing will blow over."

"I don't think so," I said. Brian's words echoed in my head. *"I didn't deserve to be lied to. . . . Dating Chris is a definite way for you to end up miserable. . . ."*

"So what did Chris say?"

I bit my lip. "Chris left."

"Well, he'll be back," Kim said, as if it were the most obvious assumption in the world.

"Right," I said doubtfully. Chris wouldn't come back. I don't know how I knew, but I was almost sure of it.

"It will all turn out okay."

I wanted to believe her. I knew she meant well, but something in my bones knew better. Somehow, I couldn't shake the feeling that this was the end of Chris and me.

The weekend dragged into a cold, rainy, lonely Monday morning, without a word from Chris.

While I was solemnly buttering my toast, Brian rushed into the kitchen and grabbed a muffin. He didn't acknowledge the fact that I was in the room. We'd managed to stay out of each other's way all weekend.

My parents had to know something was wrong—especially Mom, who knew about Chris and me—but neither of them said a word. Part of me was grateful they left Brian and me alone, but part of me wanted to run into my mother's arms and tell her everything.

"I'm late for SG," Brian announced to no one in particular. His hair was a mess and his sneakers were untied. He clearly didn't want to spend any more time than he absolutely had to in the same house with me. "Bye."

"Bye," I answered as nicely as possible. It was horrible. I'd never been uncomfortable around my own brother. To top it off, the thought of seeing Chris today made me twice as tense. But I wanted to see him. I had to know why he disappeared and never came back.

When I got to school I looked for Chris in the usual spots—near his locker, in front of the second-period chemistry lab, running late to phys. ed.—but he was nowhere to be found. The more I waited, the more I worried. Maybe he was skipping school to avoid Brian and me. But as nervous as I felt, I wasn't prepared for what I saw in the cafeteria at lunchtime.

Kim had already finished eating, but I was still picking at my french fries when I saw him. He stood by the big double doors, leaning against the wall, talking to a girl I'd never seen him with before. Chris was smiling, and she was making all these flirty gestures—touching him, giggling, flipping her hair over her shoulder. I felt as if I couldn't breathe.

"It's nothing. Just look away," Kim said, sliding her ice-cream sandwich onto my tray to entice me.

"Yeah, right," I said, my eyes glued to Chris and the girl. Chris said something and then touched her shoulder. They both laughed. *How can you laugh at a time like this?* I thought. *When Brian and I are both so hurt, how can you not care?*

"You already know he's a big flirt," Kim said.

"I suppose." I tried not to look, but I couldn't help myself.

I remembered what Brian had said about Chris being fickle. Maybe Chris *did* make every girl feel as if she were "the one," even when he didn't really love her. Maybe I was just another name on the list.

Impossible. If every girl felt as special as I did—as I had—none of them ever would have let him go. Then again, I hadn't let Chris go, but he'd gone anyway. I checked my watch. It was only noon. Three more hours left in this horrible day.

Just then, Chris gave the girl a bear hug.

Did he know I was in the room? Which would be worse—Chris flirting with someone else in front of me, or behind my back?

"Ugh," Kim said, balling her napkin and tossing it on her tray. "Let's get out of here. Next thing you know, Aaron will see that and he'll be over here asking you out." The cafeteria has only one door, so we had to pass Chris on the way.

I tried to catch his eye, but he pretended not to notice me.

"Keep walking," Kim instructed.

I gave him a small wave. No response.

At least track practice would be canceled because

142

of the rainy weather. All I wanted to do was go home, curl up in my bed, and stare at my ceiling full of stars.

"Why didn't he say something?" I asked when we were in the hallway. "Like hello. Or like, 'Lousy weather.' Is that so hard?"

"He's a coward," Kim said, taking my hand in hers as we walked. "He lied to his best friend, he treated his girlfriend like dirt, and now he's just trying to distract himself until the problem goes away."

"Including me?"

"You are the 'A Number One' reminder that he screwed up. So, yes, including you."

Kim led me into the girls' bathroom by the cafeteria and sat on the perpetually broken radiator.

"So that's it?" I felt totally helpless.

"Well, no. There's absolutely no reason why *you* shouldn't talk to *him*. After all, he is your boyfriend."

He was *my boyfriend,* I thought. We hadn't actually broken up, but obviously we weren't what we used to be. Still, Kim's words made sense. We did have something special, and no one had officially called it off, so maybe what was going on was just a bump in the road.

"It's wrong not to talk to him," I agreed. I peeled a piece of ugly orange paint off the wall, resisting the urge to add my name to the scribbled list of girls who had dated Chris.

"Right." She folded her arms across her chest as if the issue had been resolved.

"There's no reason I have to play it his way," I went on. "Avoiding. Pretending."

"You said it."

"If he's changed his mind about wanting to be with me, he should have the decency to let me know. He should give me a reason," I said, feeling stronger by the second. I crushed the paint chips into dust.

"Absolutely," Kim agreed.

"I mean, there has to be some explanation, and I'm entitled to it."

"You certainly are."

"He can't just drop out of my life without a word," I said angrily. "And at the very least, he'd be a certifiable jerk to treat his best friend's sister disrespectfully," I said.

Chris is not a jerk, I thought. Of course he'd talk to me, want to work things out. I splashed cold water on my face and took a deep breath.

"So go talk to him," Kim said, practically pushing me toward the door.

"I will," I said.

A voice inside a toilet stall cheered, "You go, girl!"

Kim and I both laughed. It felt incredibly good. Now all I had to do was go get my boyfriend back.

Twelve

I PARKED MYSELF by Chris's locker, knowing he'd have to pick up his history books after lunch. Within seconds I saw him coming. He was by himself. I don't know what I would have done if that girl from the cafeteria was with him. When he saw me, he slowed down and kind of hunched his shoulders.

All of a sudden, I felt incredibly nervous, as if I knew what lay at the end of this bumpy road was a dead end.

"Chris," I called. "Can I talk to you?"

"Hey, Dana," he said without enthusiasm. I felt the change in him immediately, but I told myself that as long as we were talking there was still hope.

"This whole thing's a mess, I know," I said quickly.

"You don't know the half of it," he spat back.

I gasped. He'd never spoken to me that way before.

"I *want* to know all of it," I said. "I mean, what's happened to us? We can barely look at each other, and three days ago we couldn't get enough of each other."

Chris nodded sadly and buried his hands in his pockets.

I kept going. "Let's drive somewhere and talk for a while. There has to be a way to work everything out."

"Listen, Dana, I think that's a bad idea," Chris said quickly. He cleared his throat and looked away.

My chest throbbed with a dull ache. "Why?"

"Well, your brother, for one thing." He sounded annoyed and looked around to make sure Brian wasn't nearby.

"I'll handle my brother," I said.

"That's not the point, Dana," Chris argued, turning back to me. "The point is that Brian and I are best buddies till the end, and no girl is worth losing your best friend over."

His words forced me to step backward. Was that all I was to him—just some girl?

Part of me understood what he meant. I wouldn't want a guy to come between Kim and me. But Chris and I had something exceptional, something I knew we could never replace. It was too important to just give up on.

"So what does that mean?" I whispered. My hand instinctively touched Chris's ID bracelet, as if it could lend me strength.

"You'll find someone else," he said, as if that

were some sort of consolation. "We both will. Someone with fewer complications. Someone without all these problems attached."

Again, I heard Brian's warning in my head. "Dating Chris is a definite way for you to end up miserable. . . . He's never been faithful to a girl." Brian had never lied to me before, and he wouldn't lie just to get back at me. And from the way Chris was acting now—so cold and unemotional—I had the awful feeling that Brian was right.

"Who was that girl you were with in the cafeteria?" I asked.

"Which girl?"

Which girl? Had there been more than one?

"The girl with the blond hair," I said, trying to keep the hurt out of my voice. "You know, the one you were talking to when you pretended you didn't see me leaving."

"Oh, Fiona? She's just a girl," Chris answered, ignoring the second part of my remark.

I wondered if that's how he would have described me to someone who asked. "Oh, Dana? She's just a girl."

Chris started to fiddle with his combination lock.

"It's just better all around if you and I forget about everything, Dana. You're a terrific girl and I had a really nice time hanging out with you, but I think we should call it off."

The words stung like pinpricks all over my body. Then, as the ache in my chest burst into full-fledged pain, Chris's words repeated and grew in my head. *"A nice time . . . a terrific girl . . . call it off."*

He opened his locker and pulled out a book. I watched him push his hair off his forehead. I knew all his gestures by heart. I loved him. How was I supposed to stop feeling that?

"It's easier this way," he went on, almost as if he were trying to convince himself. "I don't want to cause any trouble."

"Some things are worth the trouble, if you care about them," I said, hating the pleading tone of my voice. "Chris, look at me."

Chris raised his head and met my eyes directly. "I'm sorry, Dana," he said. "But I just can't deal."

What was I supposed to do? Scream at him? Hit him? Tell him I understood?

I *didn't* understand.

"Okay, Dana?" he said, his voice quiet.

"No, it's not okay," I replied. "I think you're a coward."

I turned and walked away before I could start crying. Before he had a chance to say anything in response. I didn't entirely mean it—I knew he faced a lot of things bravely in his family life—but when it came to me, he'd turned out to be a coward.

I walked around the corner and out of his sight, regretting every minute I'd spent with Chris Geller. And dreading the upcoming days without him.

"You have to let me come home with you," I told Kim after last period. I knew she had a half hour before her sister drove her to work, plenty of time to listen to me weep. We didn't talk on the way, but once we reached her house, Kim took my arm and led me to her room.

I shook my head. My expression must have said it all.

"He broke up with you?" Kim asked, shocked.

"Yeah, I guess you could say that."

Kim widened her eyes in amazement. "Are you kidding me? Did he give any explanation?"

"He said he couldn't deal." Saying the words out loud made me feel even worse. I sat on her bed, hugged my knees to my chest, and scanned the wall decorated with dance-related posters. All those ballerinas in pink satin toe shoes and filmy dresses looked so happy. I couldn't imagine feeling happy ever again.

"Couldn't deal with *you?*" Kim asked.

I shrugged, a tear sliding down my cheek. "With losing his best friend, I think. In fact, he said that no girl is worth losing your best friend over." I forced a laugh. "I guess that means I shouldn't take this personally, huh?"

Kim sank into her desk chair. She looked almost as bad as I felt.

"I can't believe Brian is splitting you guys up."

"He's not. Chris can do whatever he wants. He's not a puppet." I don't know why I felt a sudden need to defend Brian. I was still angry at him, even though now it seemed that he was right about Chris hurting me. But I had gotten the worst end

149

of the deal. Chris dumped me and Brian didn't trust me anymore. I wasn't sure which one of them I should be more angry with.

"You know," Kim said thoughtfully, "if Chris really is breaking up with you because of Brian, he's crazy. He can't turn his feelings on and off on demand. If Chris was in love with you last week, he's in love with you now. He's probably just doing what he thinks is the right thing to do. He probably doesn't *want* to break up with you."

I wanted to believe Kim in the worst way, but I remembered Chris flirting with that girl in the cafeteria and ignoring me all weekend. Worst of all, I remembered his coldhearted good-bye, and him calling me a "terrific girl," as if I were a puppy.

I shook my head.

"Talk to Brian," she suggested.

"I have. Friday night, after Chris left. All he said was that Chris doesn't treat girls very well and that I was bound to get hurt by him."

"How does *Brian* treat girls?" Kim asked.

"I don't know. He doesn't date much," I said. "Why?"

"Well . . ." Kim paused and looked at me. She still appeared pretty miserable. "The whole thing's a double shame."

"What do you mean?"

"You love Chris, and because of Brian, you can't be with him." Kim paused again.

"Right. . . ."

"And the thing is, I sort of like Brian." She looked

away from me, searching for something on her desk.

"You do?" I cried, amazed.

"Well, sort of," Kim said. "I mean, I could easily see myself going out with him."

"You two would make such an awesome couple!"

Kim gave me a little smile. "You really think we'd be good together?"

"Sure! Brian loves hanging out with you, and you guys like a lot of the same things. He's impressed with you for working after school and dancing and being so smart. . . . He wanted you to go to the movie with him Friday night, didn't he?"

"That's true," Kim said. "But it doesn't necessarily mean anything."

"It *might* mean something," I argued.

"Well, it will never happen," Kim said, crawling under the bed and emerging with a crumpled purple sweater. "Given the whole situation."

I had to admit Kim was right. Even if he were into Kim, Brian would feel too weird to do anything about it now. I mean, if he wouldn't let me date his friends, he couldn't very well start dating mine.

"I'm sorry," I said. "I guess I'm ruining things for all of us."

"Don't be silly," Kim replied, pulling the purple sweater over her head. "This isn't your fault."

"I should go home now."

"I have to get to work anyway. I'll call you," she promised.

I grabbed my bag. "I'll make sure Brian answers the phone."

What a waste, I thought as I left her house. No one could be with the person they wanted. And no matter what Kim said, I couldn't shake the feeling that the entire thing was my fault.

I got home before Brian and planted myself in front of the TV in the den.

"What are you watching?" he asked when he got home.

"Television."

"Good show?"

I nodded, trying to focus on Oprah's guests who walked in their sleep and ate everything in sight— raw meat, cigarettes, fists full of mayonnaise. But just the mention of mayonnaise reminded me of the time Chris offered me a mayonnaise snack. Even a talk show couldn't distract me. I was pathetic.

"Track practice canceled?" Brian asked.

"Rain."

"Too bad. Are you bummed?"

"Don't care." I didn't.

"Chris told me he broke up with you."

I cringed. He didn't have to say it so coldly. "He couldn't wait to tell you the good news, huh," I muttered.

"I wouldn't call it good news, Dana," he said.

"Why not?" I asked, my eyes still on the TV. "I figured you'd be relieved."

"I don't know what I am," Brian admitted. "But if you're miserable, how can I be happy?"

"Sorry," I mumbled.

"I think it's better this way," Brian said seriously.

I could tell that he was trying to help, but I still felt like punching him. How could it possibly be better without Chris?

"I mean, I just don't think it would have worked out with you two in the end," Brian went on.

"I'm sure you're right," I replied. I felt too miserable to argue with him.

"He's not reliable," Brian continued. "Eventually he would have hurt you. And it would be worse later than it is now, right?"

"Right," I said. I kept staring at the TV, but I really wasn't paying attention to what was on.

"I just hate seeing you like this," Brian said quietly.

Then why did you ruin the best thing that ever happened to me? I thought.

"It will pass," I said out loud. "I've been through worse than this, and that passed." It was true. Nothing would ever be worse than spending months in the hospital, feeling so sick I couldn't find the words to describe it. A guy dumping me— even if the guy were Chris—would never make me feel as bad as that. I guess in a strange way I'm lucky. I know I can endure whatever comes my way. This whole thing with Chris wouldn't kill me or ruin my life. I just had to wait for some of the hurt to wear away.

"I hope you feel happy again soon," Brian said.

"The only thing that would make me happy right now is if I could turn back the clock and not get involved with Chris in the first place," I told him.

"Just for the record, Dana," Brian said, standing by the doorway, "Chris seemed pretty sad too."

My first instinct was to call Chris right away, to try to help him feel better. That's what you do for people you love. But that wasn't my place anymore. Chris would have an entire lifetime of ups and downs, all of them without me.

On Tuesday, all the seniors were excused from track practice for a college fair. On Wednesday, I got excused from practice to watch Kim's dance recital. Coach Franklin was sick on Thursday, and we didn't practice on Fridays. So basically, Chris and I hardly saw each other all week. And that was fine with me.

Friday after third period, I noticed him sitting by himself on the grass near the football field. I couldn't help it. I had to see what he was doing. So I snuck up behind him, hid behind a tree, and watched. He was muttering to himself, but I couldn't hear what he said. Suddenly he slammed his palm into the ground—hard. His face reddened and he glanced down at his hand in surprise. Even from my hiding spot, I could see the blood on his palm. Chris rinsed it off with his soda. Then he shook his head, closed his eyes, and sat motionless. Hundreds of kids swarmed behind him, rushing to class, but he didn't move.

I wanted to go to him, to ask what was bothering him. But I had no right. I wasn't his girlfriend anymore. Reluctantly, I ran back inside to geometry class, where I spent the entire forty minutes staring out the window. I could see Chris in the distance. He still hadn't moved.

I sighed. There was no point in thinking about Chris any longer. He was gone for good and nothing would bring him back. But I had to take some control over my miserable life. I couldn't fix my relationship with Chris, but I could try to mend my relationship with my brother.

After all, he hadn't let me down the way Chris had. Brian was too bossy, but he did love me. And we did have to live together. I should apologize for lying to him, I realized.

Well, at least I could do something about my happiness at home.

That afternoon I came home to find Brian's legs sticking out from beneath his car. His jeans were filthy, ripped alongside his ankle, revealing a grease-stained sock.

"What'cha doing?" I asked.

"Rats!" His headless voice made it clear he'd been trying to fix something for hours.

"Need a hand?"

"Are you a mechanic?" His volume was muffled, but his sarcasm was crystal clear.

I sat on the concrete beside him. "Want a drink? Lemonade?"

"Uh-uh," he groaned. Something made a loud clanging sound.

"What broke?"

"Muffler, I think."

"Can't you take it to the shop?"

He twisted his body around so that I could see part of his face. "Care to lend me the money?"

"Chris is pretty handy with cars," I said. "Why isn't he helping you?"

Brian didn't answer.

"You two aren't talking?" I guessed.

He poked his head out and glared at me. "Don't go there, Dana."

"Right."

He disappeared again, his hand groping blindly for his wrench. I inched it closer to him and he grabbed it.

"Well, he's not talking to me either, so you have nothing to worry about."

"Great," Brian said between strange metallic squeaking sounds. "I lost a friend. You lost a—I don't know what, a boyfriend, I suppose." He overemphasized the word *boyfriend* as if it made him physically ill.

"I'm sorry," I said quietly. "For everything."

He slid himself out from under the car, threw off his gloves, sat up, and looked me in the eye.

"I'm sorry," I said again. "For lying to you and going behind your back." I swallowed back tears.

Brian studied me carefully. "You're not the only one to blame," he said.

"You mean Chris?"

"Chris. Me. You. We're all responsible. I never meant for you to get hurt, Dana."

I shrugged. "I know," I said. "But I did get hurt."

For a minute, Brian and I just stared at each other. I'd never felt so distanced from him before. No matter what we said, this Chris issue still stood between us. I couldn't think of anything to say that would make it better.

"How 'bout that lemonade?" he asked, putting on a cheerful tone.

"On its way," I said, climbing to my feet.

"Extra ice, please."

"You bet." I headed into the house.

At least some friendships—unlike Chris and Brian's—are permanent. No matter how angry Brian and I had been with each other, I knew we'd get over it in time. We would always love each other.

Even if neither of us ever made up with Chris.

I was dreading the weekend. I had no plans, and I had no boyfriend to make plans with. Things were much better with Brian—we watched TV together for a while, and sat at the dinner table like family instead of enemies. Mom didn't say anything to me, but I could tell she knew Brian and I had resolved whatever issue was tearing us apart. Given the fact that Chris hadn't been over for dinner in a long time, she probably also knew that Chris was the issue—and that we hadn't resolved anything with him.

But even though Brian and I were becoming friends again, I was still brokenhearted. Chris had taken a piece of me with him when he dumped me—a fun, loving, radiant fragment of my soul—and I couldn't imagine any way to get it back.

My mother made chicken burritos for dinner on Friday night. Brian wolfed down four, but I decorated the edge of my plate with my food instead of eating it. After Brian and I did the dishes, all I wanted was to burrow myself in my room for the rest of the night.

"You okay?" Brian asked as I trudged upstairs.

"Sad."

That was as truthful as I'd been in a long time.

An hour or so later, Brian had a visitor. I heard a car idling in the driveway and male voices having a conversation. I sat in my room in the dark, listening to the distant voices, rotating Chris's bracelet around my wrist, tracing my finger over the tiny embossed heart. Maybe I could memorize the feel of his bracelet before I gave it back to him.

Words filtered in from outside:

". . . That's not the point."

". . . I swear I'm telling you the truth."

". . . It was a rotten thing to . . ."

". . . Dana . . ."

I sprang out of bed and ran to the window. I pulled back the curtain without turning on the light.

Chris and Brian sat on the hood of Chris's Honda.

Maybe he'll ask to see me, I thought.

They laughed.

Good sign—they're getting along.

Chris handed Brian something. Then they shook hands. It looked as if they were friends again. I tried to feel happy for them, but I still wished we had told Brian the truth right away. Then Chris and Brian could have hashed this whole thing out before it got so serious. Maybe Chris and I would still be together.

Both guys stood up. I caught my breath. Was Chris coming inside?

No.

He opened his car door and for a moment the light from the car shone on his face. He hadn't shaved. He wrapped a yellow scarf loosely around his neck, and I wanted to run down and adjust it for him.

A few seconds later he was gone, driving away with my last shred of hope.

I let the curtain drop down and glanced over at my clock. Two hours until midnight. Soon it would be tomorrow, and I would have survived my first weekend night as Chris Geller's most recent ex.

I flipped on the light and began to get ready for bed.

"Dana?" Brian called softly from the hallway. He slipped a folded note beneath my door.

"I didn't read it. Don't worry," he added. I heard his footsteps fade away down the hall.

My hands shook uncontrollably, but I managed to unfold the note.

Dear Dana,

   I just wanted to let you know I'm really sorry. I didn't mean to hurt you. Please believe me. I meant everything I ever told you, but we can't be together. I'll really miss you.

Chris

I knew his words were true. He really did love me, he had never wanted to hurt me, and we would never be together again. It was a bittersweet way to make me feel better.

Before the tears could start, I unclasped his bracelet. Then I dropped it into a manila envelope and sealed it shut—a quiet, private way for me to say good-bye. Good-bye forever.

Thirteen

DANA LIPTON: GOALS
(THAT HAVE NOTHING TO DO WITH CHRIS)

—run four miles every morning before school
—volunteer at the children's cancer ward in the
    hospital
—take Kim up on her offer to teach me to
    dance
—learn karate
—get an A in biology
—try out for the swim team

"I'M HOME," BRIAN called, trotting into the kitchen. I had planted myself at the table at ten A.M. and had not moved since.

"Where have you been?" I asked. It was rare for Brian to get up, leave the house, do stuff, and come back by noon on a Saturday.

"Around. Want a sandwich?" he asked, grabbing

the gigantic jar of peanut butter my parents had bought at Costco.

"No, thanks."

"Sure? I'll make it for you."

Things between us felt almost normal. Almost.

"I'm positive. Thanks."

"What's that?" he asked, trying to read my list upside down.

"Plans," I replied, snatching it off the table.

"What did you do last night?" he asked, placing two slices of white bread in the toaster.

"Wheat bread's better for you," I said. "I stayed in my room. Reading."

"All night?"

"Yes."

The toast popped up, underdone. Brian pushed down the lever again. "Were you sick?"

"No."

"Just tired?"

"Yeah, sort of. You hashed things out with Chris last night, huh?"

"You saw us?" He looked sheepish.

"You were right outside my window," I pointed out. "How could I not?"

"Well, did you hear anything?"

"Not really. Why?" I asked suspiciously. "Is there anything you didn't want me to hear?"

"I'm not the one who keeps secrets," he said. Seeing my crestfallen expression, he added, "Sorry. I didn't mean to hit below the belt."

I shook my head. "Don't worry about it." I guess I deserved that.

"So, things are cool again with Chris and me," Brian said. "He came over and apologized and everything."

"What did you say?"

"I told him I'd known him too long to let this thing come between us, so we'd just treat it as water under the bridge. And he totally agreed."

Great. To Chris and Brian, I was just "this thing." I was merely water under the bridge. How nice.

"I'm happy for you," I told Brian. But I couldn't help feeling bitter at the same time.

"And then I came up with a surefire plan to cheer you up," Brian went on. "Because you've been in such a major funk, and it's partly my fault, I figure it's the least I can do. Here," he said, handing me a small envelope he'd taken out of his back pocket. "My treat."

"What is it?" I asked.

"Take a look."

In the envelope was a third-row seat for a Scorching Stones concert, Saturday, November 4. I couldn't believe it.

"This is for tonight! How did you get this?" I said, amazed. I hadn't even known they were playing in Atlanta again. I wondered if Chris knew. . . .

I quickly pushed that thought out of my head.

"I bought it, genius." Brian laughed. "One for you, one for me. I was lucky. I got the last two seats, and they're really good ones."

"But you hate the Scorching Stones," I protested. "You're always telling me how much they stink!"

"But *you* love them, and I'm trying to cheer you up," he said. "So you'll have fun and maybe I'll change my mind about them. Bands always sound better live."

"This was really thoughtful of you," I said quietly, clutching the ticket. "Really."

"I'm going to be at the library all afternoon, so I'll just meet you at the concert," he said. "Mom already said she could drive you there, okay? How does that sound?"

"Sounds good. I'll meet you out in front?"

"No way. It will be impossible for us to find each other in the crowds. Let's just meet at our seats." He shoved a huge bite of toasted peanut butter sandwich in his mouth and disappeared upstairs.

Of course I wanted to go to the Scorching Stones concert. Especially since it was a peace gesture from Brian. But at the same time, just thinking about the band brought back so many memories of Chris—from the CDs he played in his car to our intense night after the last concert. Now even my favorite music was inseparable from my love for him.

But my relationship with Brian needed taking care of too. It would be good for my brother and me to have a fun night together.

"I hear you scored seats to the Scorching Stones concert," Kim said enviously. I was in the middle of throwing every article of clothing I owned onto the bedroom floor when she arrived.

"Yeah. Pretty cool, huh," I said blandly, trying to convey to her how meaningless it all felt given my recent history with Chris. Kim was unfazed.

"You should go, definitely. Definitely, you have to go!" Kim spoke with so much enthusiasm, I couldn't believe she was talking about my date with my brother.

"Of course I'm going," I said, squeezing into a pair of old shrunken jeans.

"They're too tight on you," she said, sitting on the floor and stretching.

"Thanks a lot."

"I'm not saying you're fat," she added. "It's just that those jeans don't really fit."

"Quit while you're ahead," I said, forcing the pants off my thighs.

"I know you'll have an awesome time," she told me.

She seemed pretty worked up about the whole thing. I suppose she felt like Brian—that I'd been moping for long enough.

"The music will be good anyway," I said. "I'm sorry it's not you going with Brian."

Kim shook her head. "Don't even think about that. Just have a good time," she said.

I nodded. I would try to have fun, then it would be over, and I'd be relieved.

"Wear a skirt," Kim commanded as I tried on a pair of black leggings.

"Why?"

"Skirts make everyone feel better," Kim proclaimed.

I started to protest, then stopped. Why not? I'd felt so crummy for so long, maybe a skirt *would* put me in a better mood. It was a Saturday night after all, and even though my big brother was hardly my first choice for a date, there was no reason to look dingy. Maybe I'd meet some amazing guy at the concert.

The thought depressed me. I didn't want anyone but Chris.

I put on the skirt I'd bought at Kim's store and added a silky white blouse. I even wore a little makeup, just enough eyeliner and mascara to make my eyes look bigger, and some natural-looking pinkish matte lipstick.

"Here," Kim said, removing her turquoise and sterling silver earrings. "Wear these."

"Really?"

She inserted them into my earlobes. "They bring out the green in your eyes."

I heard my mom start the car as I took one final look in the mirror. I stuck my lipstick in my purse and said to Kim, "I am going to have fun tonight. Tonight, I am going to have fun."

Kim smiled. "Tonight, Dana Lipton, you are going to have the time of your life!"

I waited eagerly in my seat for Brian to arrive. In spite of my bad mood, the atmosphere in the arena was exciting. It was hard to be unhappy when I was surrounded by so many screaming, laughing people. The place was jammed. A group of kids from my high school was singing one of the band's songs at the top of their lungs. Pretty soon some kids from our rival high school told them to shut up. They got into a war of insults. It was so much fun I didn't even see someone take Brian's seat.

"Dana?"

I jumped and turned around.

Chris sat next to me, looking bewildered.

"What are *you* doing here?" I cried, panicked. *And what girl did you bring with you this time?* I thought.

"Brian got tickets for him and me. What are *you* doing here?"

"You're here with Brian?" I narrowed my eyes.

"Yeah," Chris explained, his face still a little pale. "He said he was sorry he'd gotten so burned up at me, so this was a peace offering."

"But Brian got me a ticket to cheer—" I was about to say "cheer me up," but I didn't want to let Chris know how upset I'd been. "—to clear the air between him and me. He didn't tell you I was coming?"

"No," Chris said. "Did he tell you I was coming?"

"No!"

We stared at each other silently for a moment.

Then Chris smiled and the color returned to his face. "It's a setup," he said. "Don't you get it?"

"Brian set us up?" I whispered doubtfully.

Chris's smile grew wider. He reached over and took my hand, squeezing it with excitement. I wanted to squeeze back. Would we have a second chance to be together?

I was afraid to hope.

A voice boomed over the loudspeaker, announcing Atlanta's one and only Scorching Stones. The crowd screamed and whistled. Chris kept talking to me, but I couldn't hear him over the noise. Then the band came on, blaring its electric guitars, and the audience went wild.

Chris leaned over to kiss me, and all my fear began to fade. But when his lips touched mine, something in me rebelled. I pulled away. His words came rushing back to me: *"I had a really nice time hanging out with you."* His voice had been so cold when he broke up with me, and it seemed so easy for him to do. The note he gave me last night said he still cared, but how could I trust him?

Chris stood up and grabbed my hand. "Let's get out of here," he yelled. He dragged me out of my seat, pushing us through the row full of dancing fans. I pictured Chris's face as he said, "You're a terrific girl" and "I can't deal with this." How could I fit the guy who'd spoken those words with the guy who seemed to love and want me back?

"Why would Brian set us up together?" I asked when we found a secluded corner in the lobby. "He never wanted us together."

Chris held my hands in his. "Last night," he

said, "I came over to your place, to apologize to Brian. . . ."

"I know, I know. You apologized for dating me. You two are best friends again. I'm water under the bridge."

". . . and to ask him to give you a letter. Did he?"

I nodded.

"I was afraid you hated me, that you were so mad at me I'd have no chance of even getting you to hear me out."

"You might have been right," I admitted.

"When I gave Brian the letter for you, he told me I looked like a mess."

I laughed. "And you said?"

"I said I *felt* like a mess."

"Why?"

"Where do I start?" Chris looked at the wall as if it might give him the answer. Then he put his hands on my shoulders and gazed into my eyes. "Nothing's fun anymore. Running, basketball, eating, hanging out—all of it—I hate everything. I hate myself for lying to Brian and hurting a really tight friendship. I hate being without you. I hate having hurt you. I hate myself for having asked you to lie to Brian."

Chris's eyes filled with tears. "I was really scared I'd wrecked your relationship with your brother. I kept thinking about that story you told me, about the night he sat by your bed in the hospital and vowed always to take care of you. I couldn't believe I'd messed up that relationship."

"You said all this to Brian?"

"No," Chris admitted. "What I said was that I loved you and that I didn't want to lose you. But that nothing in the world was more valuable to me than his friendship, and I was sorry I'd betrayed him."

"And he said?"

"He said he was impressed. Can you believe it? For weeks I acted like a jerk, and Brian said he was impressed because I apologized. Then he said he needed some time to think things through. When he called this morning and said he had these tickets, I thought he was making a pretty cool gesture of friendship. But I never thought he'd do *this!*"

I wondered why Brian hadn't told me what he and Chris really talked about. I remembered his rush to get out of the kitchen after he made himself a sandwich this morning, the way he told me to meet him at our seats instead of out front. The whole time, he must have been planning this setup—planning to get Chris and me back together. I felt a huge rush of love for my brother. He'd been so worried about Chris hurting me. He'd been so intent on protecting me from that. But this was his way of admitting that he'd been wrong. It was his way of saying he knew my love life was something I had to deal with for myself. I knew how hard it must have been for Brian to stop trying to take care of me.

"Dana," Chris said quietly, "I miss you so much I don't know what to do with myself. But I couldn't keep doing something I knew really upset him."

"Me neither," I agreed.

"But it looks like Brian's given us the go-ahead. Now it's up to you, Dana. Are *you* willing to give us a second chance?"

I didn't know what to say. Brian had been right about one thing—Chris really did hurt me a lot. Did I want to risk being hurt again?

Chris waited a moment for my reply, and when I remained frozen he took a piece of notebook paper out of his pocket and unfolded it.

"I wrote you another letter, but I was too afraid to give it to you," he confessed.

I held out my hand. "Can I see?"

He pulled back. "Well, I'm not sure. Now I feel sort of funny." Suddenly shy, he refolded the letter and put it away. He leaned forward, his lips close to mine. "Give us another try, Dana. Please. And if you can't, at least say you won't hate me."

"*Hate* you?" I repeated, tears welling in my eyes. My throat felt tight. "How can I hate you when I love you so much?"

I moved forward, and Chris's lips were on mine, kissing me as if we'd been separated for a lifetime.

Fourteen

WE DECIDED TO leave the concert and go straight to my house to thank Brian. We figured he'd be waiting for us anyway, eager to hear what happened. But neither of us expected to see him sitting on the couch, holding hands with Kim!

"Congratulations!" Kim cheered.

"Well, congratulations to you too, I guess!" I said.

"You knew about this whole plan?" Chris asked, shocked.

She beamed at him. "I told Dana she'd have a really awesome time at the concert."

"Thanks for the tickets, Bri—and for everything else," Chris said.

"Glad it worked out," he replied with a big smile.

"But you were so against our being together," I said to my brother.

"Don't remind him of his old and stupid ways," Kim joked.

"It's true," Brian admitted. "I was against it at first. But you were a total disaster without Chris, and Chris was totally depressed without you, so I figured you two must have had something pretty special going on after all."

"We do," Chris and I said in unison.

"Besides, I realized that if you told me I wasn't allowed to go out with Kim, I'd be pretty angry." Brian put his arm around Kim.

"I know you meant well," I said. "You were only trying to take care of me."

"But I took things too far. Although if you treat my sister the way you treated your other girlfriends, you'll have to answer to me," he told Chris.

I glanced up at Chris and raised my eyebrows questioningly. Brian had a good point.

Chris looked a little uncomfortable. "I've never had a girlfriend like Dana," he said, glancing at me. "I'm in love with her—how could I treat her badly?"

My heart swelled with happiness and Brian nodded. "Okay, then. And as for the lying thing," he continued, "I still wish you hadn't, but I kind of understand why you did. I was sort of, you know, inflexible."

"Really?" Kim said, winking at me.

"Did *you* have something to do with Brian changing his mind?" I asked her.

"Well, it really was all Brian's idea. I just tried to

173

reassure him that he was doing the right thing. For all four of us."

I liked the sound of that, and obviously Brian did too. He kissed Kim's cheek and she smiled.

"Dana and I are thirsty," Kim announced.

"Okay, I get it. Girl-talk time," Brian said, standing up.

Chris and Brian headed to the kitchen to grab some sodas, and Kim answered my question before I could ask it.

"Tonight," she said. "Nothing went on before then, I swear."

"How did it happen?" I asked happily.

"Brian came by my house this morning to ask me if I thought you and Chris really loved each other, and I told him I'd never seen your face light up the way it did when you talked about Chris. That really hit home with him, and he told me he didn't want to stand in the way of your happiness."

"And you said?" I prompted.

"I told him you'd need a little push to get back together with Chris, and that's when he decided to do the whole concert setup. And then, he asked me to hang out with him tonight."

"And?" I said eagerly.

"And, well, we talked for a while." Kim peeked into the kitchen. The guys were goofing around with the ice-cube tray. "About you and Chris and sophomores and seniors, me and him, stuff like that."

"Yes, and?" I was impatient now, wondering who had made the first move.

"And then your brother sort of, well, asked if he could kiss me."

What a gentleman! I had no idea Brian would be so old-fashioned.

"And so I said yes, of course." Kim blushed.

I grinned.

"And so," she continued, "that's that."

"No way. That's just the beginning," I told her as Chris and Brian appeared with sodas and chips for us all.

Kim and Brian would make an excellent couple. I was sure of it.

There were now two happiest nights of my life, I thought as I scanned all the joyful faces in the room. The first—when the doctors told me the bone marrow transplant had worked and I didn't have cancer anymore. The second—being reunited with Chris.

An hour after Kim and Chris went home that night, Chris called to me from outside my window. I had just put his bracelet back on my wrist, and it made me feel special and loved. I was glad I had never returned it. I knew I should have, but maybe some tiny part of me had known that Chris and I were meant to be.

The sky was blue-black, the stars brighter and far more mysterious than they had seemed all week. I leaned over my window ledge and blew him a kiss.

"Be careful—people will think you're a burglar," I said, giggling.

"No burglar hovers around people's houses and leaves notes," he said. "I put something through the mail slot in your front door. Better go get it before someone else does."

"Don't go anywhere," I commanded. I scrambled out of my room and ran as quickly and quietly as I could down the steep carpeted stairs. I found a folded piece of notebook paper on the doormat. On the front, Chris had scribbled, "The Real Letter." I opened it.

2 A.M.

Dear Dana,

First of all, I love you. Second of all, I wish I could find a way to tell you. And third of all, letting you go was the biggest mistake of my life.

"My dreams run strong and far when I'm with you. . . ."

The Bone Marrow Donors Registry called today to tell me I'm a potential match. Next week I go in for more tests to be sure.

I asked for information about the patient, but as you know it's all done anonymously, so I'm not allowed to know many details. All they told me is that the patient is a teenage girl suffering from advanced Hodgkin's disease. Right now there's a

95% chance she'll die. A bone marrow transplant is the only thing that could save her life.

She'll never know anything about me, or the fact that she has you to thank, because I never would have registered if it weren't for you. Together, we might be able to save someone's life.

It looks like our secret love might have been a miracle.

Love always (I mean that literally),
Chris

I grabbed Brian's jean jacket off the coatrack, threw it over my shoulders, and stepped outside. A hint of winter and the excitement of renewed love made me shiver. I saw Chris standing on my doorstep. I realized, as we looked at each other with wonder, that the pain of the past really can be put to good use. And that the future—Chris's, mine, and that of a dying stranger—was just about to begin.

Do you ever wonder about falling in love? About members of the opposite sex? Do you need a little friendly advice but have no one to turn to? Well, that's where we come in . . . Jenny and Jake. Send us those questions you're dying to ask, and we'll give you the straight scoop on life and love in the nineties.

DEAR JAKE

Q: *I had a crush on my best friend's brother, Danny, for years. So I was really happy when he finally asked me out and we started dating. My friend is totally fine with it. She even likes us being together. However, I don't know if I like him anymore and I kind of want to break up with him. I'm afraid my best friend will kill me if I hurt Danny. How can I get out of this?*

JK, Allentown, PA

A: If your friend is psyched about this relationship, she might be disappointed when it doesn't work out. However, she probably respects her brother's and your right to your own lives, and that's why she never interfered in the first place.

No matter how your friend really feels, there are still things you can do for damage control.

First, be gentle with Danny. Comments such as "I've realized I'm just not attracted to you" or "I've decided I'd rather date someone intelligent" are definitely out. Remember that if you intend to stay close with your best friend, you'll be running into Danny a lot in the future, so you should leave things as pleasant as possible. Hopefully your friend is mature enough to accept whatever happens between you and Danny without letting it affect your friendship.

Q: *I dated Reuben for a couple of weeks, but the chemistry wasn't there. The breakup wasn't bad, and we stayed friends. Recently I met a friend of his, Steve, and we hit it off. Now I'm just not sure what to do. Is it okay to date Reuben's friend? I don't want to feel like a hot potato or anything, and I wouldn't want to hurt Reuben. What's the etiquette for these situations?*

JC, Chevy Chase, MD

A: I'll tell you one thing—if it were as easy as telling you which fork you use to eat the salad and which one you use for the main course, we'd be in business. Unfortunately, there's no tried-and-true way to get through dating dilemmas such as yours. There are, however, certain helpful hints. For instance, how strong are your feelings for Steve and his for you? If you sense the potential for a lasting relationship here, it's worth fighting for. Since you claim that both you and Reuben realized that friendship worked best for you two, he shouldn't mind your dating someone else. He might be a little hurt that you found a connection with his friend when you couldn't find it with him, but he'll probably get past that.

In the end, you'll have to weigh the risks and benefits and decide what seems best for everyone involved. It sounds like you're sensitive enough to do the right thing.

Q: *My friends call me Fickle Frannie, because I never stay with one guy for very long. When I first meet someone, I fall head over heels and think I've finally found the guy for me. Then after a couple of weeks I always find things wrong with him, and I move on. I want a long relationship, but I can't seem to find the right guy. Am I just too picky?*

FS, Longboat Key, FL

A: It's important to respect yourself enough to use discretion when you date. You have high standards for the guy who can win your heart, and that's great. However, you didn't specify what kinds of problems you find with these guys. It's one thing if they start breaking dates or calling you by their ex-girlfriends' names. It's quite another thing if the disqualifying features you're noticing include such things as "His hair's an inch too long" or "I don't like the way he laughs."

If the reasons you're dumping these guys are minor, maybe you don't want a relationship as much as you think you do. There's no rush—enjoy dating for a while without commitment. Just make sure that when you're ready to get serious you realize that no one is perfect and you probably have some annoying little habits of your own that your boyfriend will find as endearing as you will learn to find his.

DEAR JENNY

Q: *I've been friends with Rick since we were in fourth grade, and now we're both sixteen. During all these years he always said he liked me, but I never felt the same way about him. Now I notice myself getting jealous when he talks to other girls and I don't know what to feel. Could I be falling for him?*

MP, Austin, TX

A: Matters of the heart are never clear. You're learning just how confusing emotions can be. You know that Rick means a lot to you, but you're not sure if he's *the one* or just a close friend.

Before you make any decisions, ask yourself some questions. Is your sudden interest in Rick coming from your jealousy of not getting all his attention anymore? Rick cares deeply for you, and I'm sure that no matter whom he dates, your friendship will still be important to him. On the other hand, are you genuinely upset at the idea of him dating another girl? Have you caught yourself daydreaming about what it would be like to kiss him? If the feelings you're having for Rick are sincere, go ahead and give it a try—he could be the perfect guy for you.

Q: *My boyfriend, Jack, likes to be very affectionate in public. When we go places, he holds my hand, puts his arm around me, and sometimes even kisses me! I really love Jack and when we're alone I love kissing him, but I'm just uncomfortable touching him like that in front of other people. Is there something wrong with me?*

AK, Tucson, AZ

A: There's nothing wrong with you at all; everyone has their own opinions about PDA (public displays of affection) and your feelings are as valid as the next person's. Jack wants to show you how much he cares, so he makes an effort to be close to you at all times. You, however, want to express your feelings in a more private setting, without an audience.

What you have to do is let Jack know that although you enjoy his kisses, you really don't want the rest of the world to enjoy watching them. Be sure to make him understand that he hasn't done anything wrong; you'd just rather do things a little differently. And maybe you can compromise: Hold his hand once in a while, but save the more intimate moments for later.

Q: *I've been in a serious relationship with Gene for two years, and now I'm moving to a different city. I love him very much and he loves me, so we don't want to break up. But I'm worried that maybe we shouldn't have this kind of commitment if we're going to live far away from each other. We're only seventeen and we've never really dated other people. What should I do?*

LH, Minneapolis, MN

A: You're certainly very young to commit yourself to one person who you won't be able to see very often. It's possible that once you move, you'll meet new people and want to experience the dating scene. Be prepared that you and Gene both might feel this way. It's also possible that your feelings for each other are strong enough to last long distance, and neither of you will be attracted to anyone new. What's important is simply that you recognize that either of these situations could occur, and it's hard to predict how you'll feel until the time comes. Above all, be true to your own emotions no matter what you think you "should" be doing. Your heart will tell you what the right choice is.

Do you have questions about love? Write to:

Jenny Burgess or Jake Korman
c/o Daniel Weiss Associates
33 West 17th Street
New York, NY 10011

Real *life.*
Real *friends.*
Real *faith.*

Introducing Clearwater Crossing—

where friendships are formed, hearts
come together, choices have consequences,
and lives are changed forever . . .

#1   0-553-57118-4

#2   0-553-57121-4

laura peyton roberts

Bantam Doubleday Dell
Books for Young Readers

BFYR 160

Watch out
Sweet Valley
University—
the Wakefield
twins are
on campus!

Jessica and Elizabeth are away
at college, with no parental
supervision! Going to classes
and parties . . . learning about
careers and college guys . . .
they're having the time of their
lives. Join your favorite twins as
they become SVU's favorite coeds!

Look for
the SVU series
wherever
books are
sold.